During the song service, Charles was hard put to concentrate on the songs.

His glance kept going to Olivia at the piano. Now, why couldn't he keep his eyes off her? It was true she was pretty, with her reddish-gold curls peeking out from beneath the tiny hat atop her head. And when she glanced up, the blue of her eyes sparkled like sapphires. But he and Livvy had never been more than friends. She was like a younger sister to him.

Feeling a little dazed, he gave his head a quick shake and looked down at the hymnbook. He peered at the page, opened his mouth and his loud baritone swelled out with the words "Shall we gather at the river, where bright angel feet have trod." A giggle from the girls seated in front of him and the incredulous frown from the song leader was his first indication something was wrong.

Little by little it seeped into his head and ears that the congregation was singing "Rescue the Perishing."

With an embarrassed attempt at an apologetic smile, Charles found the correct page and cleared his throat before joining in. His burning ears were a sure sign his face was red as a ripe tomato.

FRANCES DEVINE

grew up in the great state of Texas, where she wrote her first story at the age of nine. She moved to south-west Missouri more than twenty years ago and fell in love with the hills, the fall colors and Silver Dollar City. Frances has always loved to read, and considers herself blessed to have the opportunity to write in her favorite genre. Frances is the mother of seven adult children and has fourteen wonderful grandchildren.

FRANCES DEVINE

A Touch of Autumn

HEARTSONG
PRESENTS

Recycling programs for this product may not exist in your area.

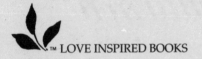

™ LOVE INSPIRED BOOKS

ISBN-13: 978-0-373-48661-8

A TOUCH OF AUTUMN

www.LoveInspiredBooks.com

Printed in U.S.A.

But Jesus said, "Permit little children,
and forbid them not, to come unto me;
for of such is the kingdom of heaven."
—*Matthew* 19:14

This book is dedicated with appreciation and respect to all the teachers who helped my deaf-blind son, Jack Schultz, through the years.

To the school in Colorado Springs, built due to a measles epidemic that had left many children blind. Although Jack was with you for only a few months while awaiting a slot to open elsewhere, you gave him his start and it was very helpful.

To the Alabama Institute for the Deaf-Blind in Talladega. It was rough sometimes, but thanks to the teachers there, Jack had doors opened we could hardly imagine. There he learned sign language, Braille and living skills. Thanks so much for all you did.

And to the Helen Keller school on Long Island. I know there were some bad experiences because Jack wanted to be at home, but you were kind to him and took good care of him while he was there.

To teachers everywhere, I know it's tough sometimes, but don't give up. You're doing a great job.

To my children, I know it wasn't always easy, but thank you for loving your brother and helping with his care.

And to Jack, I love you so much. What would I do without you?

Chapter 1

Georgia, September 1893

"There you go, Miss Olivia. That's the last of it." Rudy Baker rubbed his hands on his overalls then stepped back and turned mournful brown eyes on Olivia Shepherd.

Oh, dear. Surely he wasn't still carrying a torch for her. Olivia dropped her gaze to the list Pa had given her, then matched each item with the goods Rudy had loaded in the wagon.

"Thanks, Rudy." She gave him a hint of a smile. No sense in giving him any ideas. He was handsome enough, but… She sighed and climbed up on the seat.

If only Charles Waverly would look at her the way Rudy did, maybe he'd see her as something besides a sisterly, old-maid friend. She huffed. Twenty-six wasn't so old, but you'd think it was ancient from some of the whispered remarks she'd overheard from time to time.

Well, she could tell the gossipy old women a thing or two. She'd probably had as many, if not more, offers of courtship and marriage as anyone else in the community.

She blinked back a tear as she guided the mules toward the edge of Magnolia Junction. The problem was that she didn't want any of those prospective suitors. If she couldn't have Charles, she'd just as soon stay at the parsonage with Ma and Pa forever.

"Olivia, hello!"

Olivia glanced to her left and reined in the mules. Helen Flannigan stood on the boardwalk that lined the left side of the square with her eleven-year-old stepdaughter, Molly. Great. More salt in the wound.

"Hello, Helen, Molly. Awfully hot to be out walking. Can I take you somewhere before I leave town?"

"No, we're meeting Patrick at the hotel for ice cream." Helen shaded her eyes against the late-morning sun. "We'd be happy if you'd join us."

"Oh, thanks. I'd love to, but I have to get home and help Mama with dinner. Besides, I have a few perishable items." She motioned over her shoulder to the supplies in back.

"All right. See you at church on Sunday, then." Helen waved and continued down the street with Molly.

With a flick of the reins, Olivia urged the mules forward. She really had to get over the kicked-in-the-stomach feeling she got every time she saw Helen. After all, it wasn't the teacher's fault that Charles had fallen in love with her. Or thought he had. It was no one's fault. A long sigh made its way from deep inside her. Just as it was no one's fault that Olivia had fallen head over heels in love with Charles six years ago when he came to teach at Cecilia Quincy School for the Deaf. One glance into his laughing, brown eyes and she was done for.

She still felt guilt over the relief that had washed over her when Helen turned him down and married Patrick Flannigan. Shouldn't she have felt grief for Charles instead? Especially when he'd unloaded his sorrows on her for nearly two weeks. Which, of course, was more proof that he'd never thought of Olivia as anything but a friend.

Tightening her lips, she focused on her driving. She had no intention of falling into a pit of despair today like some schoolgirl mooning over a boy. She'd rather enjoy the live oaks and magnolias she drove past. She smiled when the road curved around a small pond and the weathered frame church and parsonage came into view. They needed a fresh coat of paint, but Olivia's heart filled at the sight anyway. Home.

She urged the mules around to the back door of the house and reined them in. As she climbed down from the wagon, Jake, the hired hand, walked over from the barn.

"How was your trip into town, Miss Olivia?" Jake shoved his hat back from his wrinkled forehead, and shot her a friendly grin.

"Oh, same as usual. I bought plenty of grain for the chickens this time."

"That's good. We were a little short last month." He grabbed a crate and headed for the house, not mentioning the fact that Olivia had knocked over last month's container of chicken feed, spilling at least a third of it. Once the house supplies were all unloaded, he waved and climbed in the wagon to take the rest of the supplies to the barn.

Olivia's mother came into the large, comfortable kitchen. "Did you see anyone we know in town today, dear?"

Olivia smiled as she gave her mother a hug and kiss. Hannah Shepherd's face was as smooth as Olivia's, except for the laugh lines around her eyes.

"Mr. and Mrs. Baker, of course, and Rudy." She grabbed a pair of scissors and snipped the thread on the bag of flour. "Oh, and I saw Helen and Molly."

"That's nice." Mama pushed the big lard bucket into a corner. "I wonder if the deaf school has found anyone to replace her."

"Abigail said Helen plans to continue teaching for a while." She emptied the flour into the bin, taking careful aim, but it still rained a shower of white all over her.

"Why, that's scandalous! A married woman's place is in the home."

Olivia shrugged. "I guess she doesn't think so. And Patrick's allowing it, so he must not care."

Her mother frowned. "At least Molly will be in school all day. I'm sure Helen won't teach once she's..." Her face turned pink and she turned away, bustling around the supplies. "We should have plenty of sugar and flour for the baking now. I promised chocolate cakes and custard and apple pies. So we'll be busy this week."

Olivia hid a grin that Mama would think it improper to mention someone in the family way to her unmarried daughter. "And cookies. Don't forget that you promised oatmeal-raisin cookies."

"Yes." Mama sighed. "And that doesn't count the fried chicken and potato salad. I'm not sure combining the Labor Day picnic with the back-to-school celebration is such a good idea. It's an awful lot of work."

"I can't see that it matters, Mama. If we held them separately, everyone would come to both anyway. So we'd still have the same amount of work, only twice."

"You're right of course. Oh, Olivia. I forgot. Charles dropped by while you were in town. He seemed quite disappointed to find you gone."

* * *

Charles Waverly loved everything about Quincy School. The smell of the polished wood floors, the joy on a student's face when a difficult assignment was completed well, the satisfying camaraderie with the other teachers. But what he loved the most was the first week of September.

Luggage, students and parents overflowed the large foyer and spilled onto the grand staircase. Laughter reverberated to the high ceilings and reached into the farthest rooms, with an occasional reprimand from an anxious father wanting his son or daughter to make a good impression.

A scream rent the air and Helen's stepdaughter, Molly, and her friend Trudy ran to greet a new arrival. Here and there a group of two or three friends stood together, their hands moving rapidly in sign language as they greeted each other after the long vacation.

Tantalizing aromas drifted from the kitchen, where Selma the cook and her assistants worked their magic. He was almost certain he smelled gumbo as well as Cook's famous fried chicken.

A bundle of energy and laughter in the form of an eight-year-old boy barreled into him, grabbing him around the waist. "Mr. Charles. Did you miss me? I sure missed you."

The high tones of the boy's voice sent joy running through Charles. When Sonny had first come to Quincy, he knew no speech at all.

Charles laughed and returned the boy's hug. "Of course I missed you, Sonny. There was no one around to plant frogs in my chair."

Sonny giggled. "Do you think Cook is making peach cobbler for dessert? I ain't tasted any since school was out." He glanced around and waved to a boy across the foyer.

Charles grinned and with one finger gently turned Sonny's face back toward him. "*Haven't* tasted any, not *ain't.*" Amazing how even deaf children still managed to pick up poor English habits. He ruffled the boy's hair. "And I'm almost certain she wouldn't have left out everyone's favorite dessert."

Sonny spotted Helen coming down the hall from the director's office and, with a quick goodbye, he ran off to greet her.

It had taken Charles a while to get over his embarrassment around Helen after he'd made a fool of himself proposing last year, but she went out of her way to put him at ease. Now, they were friends again. He must have gone a little crazy for a while to think what he'd felt for her was love. He still wasn't quite sure what it had been. Maybe Trent and Abigail Quincy's wedding and obvious joy the year before had something to do with it. Or maybe just seeing his dear friend Helen giving her attention to another man had made him jealous. But, oh, how he thanked God she'd turned him down and married Patrick Flannigan.

He was delighted at their obvious happiness. But Charles was quite sure wedded bliss wasn't for him. He planned to stay single and focus his attention on his students. The only woman he had any tender feelings for was Livvy, who was like the little sister he never had.

The thought of Livvy made him grin. She could always make him laugh without even trying. He didn't know what he'd have done without her those first few weeks after Helen had gently but firmly refused his proposal of courtship and marriage. Too bad Olivia hadn't been at home yesterday when he'd stopped by. But he'd see her at church on Sunday.

"Ow!" A child's cry of pain drew Charles's attention. He glanced up. Jeremiah, one of the older students, grinned as Sonny limped away. Was that boy going to be a problem again? They'd just about cured him of bullying last year, but it looked as if he'd returned to his old tricks over the summer.

Charles headed across the room and touched Sonny's arm, getting his attention. "What's wrong?"

"Nothing. I just tripped." Sonny ducked his head. "May I go now, Mr. Charles?"

"Yes, of course. But, Sonny, if someone is picking on you, you need to let me know. Or one of the other teachers."

"Yes, sir." Sonny scooted across the room and up the stairs.

Charles sighed. Just like last year. The younger children were either afraid to report any bullying or didn't want to be pegged as tattletales. And Jeremiah was too smart to be easily caught. Charles tightened his lips. This behavior had to be stopped right away. He had no intention of allowing the children to be miserable all year.

"Well, there he go again." Virgie, the thin, elderly housekeeper who ran the household staff with a firm but gentle hand, patted him on the shoulder. "Don't you worry none, Mr. Charles. That boy just need someone to care about him. And I know you be the one who can do that."

He gave her a tender smile and sighed. "I hope so, Virgie. I hope so."

Her wrinkled, brown hand gave him another pat, then she walked toward the kitchen area.

Charles stepped out on the porch and leaned against one of the pillars. The vast lawn boasted a magnolia tree on each side of the walkway. He could almost smell the lemony fragrance they'd emitted during spring and early summer. But the blossoms were long gone. He inhaled, thankful for the breeze today.

But what could he do about Jeremiah? Maybe he and

Livvy could put their heads together. She was Sonny's Sunday school teacher and the child was one of her favorites.

But it was disappointing to see Jeremiah revert to his old ways. Virgie was right. Something must be troubling the boy to cause that sort of behavior. If only he could find a way to find out what that something was.

Chapter 2

Batter splashed over the rim of the cream-colored bowl and dripped down the side. Olivia gasped and quickly scraped the gooey chocolate back into the bowl. She'd done it again. Let her daydreams distract her. She took a deep breath. A lock of hair fell across her eyes and she used the back of her hand to swipe it out of the way.

"Livvy, dear, I think that cake is mixed enough. You're going to beat too much air into it and ruin the texture." Mama smiled. "Here, I'll hold the pans steady while you pour."

"Thanks, Mama." She straightened and tried to focus on the simple task of pouring batter into cake pans.

Mama's gentle spirit shone on her countenance as she sent a questioning look at her daughter. "What's bothering you?"

"Oh, nothing, Mama."

"Very well, Livvy, dear. But if you'd like to talk about

it, you know I'm always willing to listen." She glanced at Olivia. "Who knows? I may even have a little wisdom for you."

Olivia bent over and placed the filled cake pans in the oven. When she straightened, she gave her mother what she hoped was a convincing smile. "Thank you, but I'm really perfectly fine. Nothing's wrong at all."

"Hmm." A raised brow proved that Olivia wasn't fooling her mother, but she nodded. "All right, then. Do you think we have enough baked goods for the picnic?" She glanced in the cupboard that stood against the back wall. Pies and cakes, covered with tea towels, lined the shelves, ready for the Labor Day picnic, just two days away.

Olivia smiled and laid her hand on her mother's arm. "Mama, there are more than enough cakes and pies even if no one else makes anything. And we still have cookies to bake."

Laughter pealed through Mama's lips. "I do get carried away sometimes. I think we'll have one of the pies for dessert tomorrow. Did you invite Charles for Sunday dinner?"

"No, I'm sure he'll need to have dinner at the school. This is the students' first Sunday back at school and some of the parents will stay over until Monday."

"Oh, of course. I don't know what I was thinking. Did he say whether all the students returned this year?"

"I haven't seen him since last Sunday." She wouldn't see him as much now that school was starting. No more lazy afternoon walks. No more picnic lunches by the river. She bit her lip and focused her attention on what her mother was saying.

"I guess we'll see for ourselves at church tomorrow." Mama patted Olivia on the shoulder. "We'd better fix something for your father to eat for his supper before we bake the cookies."

"Mama, why don't you go to the parlor and put your feet up for a while. I'll warm up the leftover stew. You've been working hard all day and it's going to be late when we finish our baking."

Mama frowned and gave Olivia an uncertain glance. "But I meant to make hot biscuits to go with the stew."

"I'll make them. I don't mind at all."

"Well…if you're sure. I could do with a breather."

"I'm sure." Olivia smiled and kissed her mother on the cheek. "I'll call you and Papa when supper's ready."

Charles tried to focus on the reverend's sermon, but his gaze kept drifting to Jeremiah, who sat in front of him and right next to Sonny.

Jeremiah had only been at Quincy since the previous year and had had no prior formal education. He'd had trouble learning signs, but his lip-reading had improved since his mother had enrolled him. Perhaps, as his communication skills improved, his attitude would, too. The bullying could simply be an outlet for his frustration. If only something could be done before the boy got himself expelled.

Charles stood with the congregation and sang the deeply moving hymn, "Just As I Am." When Reverend Shepherd prayed the closing prayer, Charles added his own silent petition that God would give him the wisdom to help Jeremiah.

When he stepped out of the church, he spotted Olivia standing across the churchyard with Abigail Quincy and walked over. He tipped his hat. "Ladies."

Abigail grinned and cut a glance from him to Olivia. "Well, I need to go rescue my baby. She was being passed around hand to hand a few minutes ago."

Charles frowned as she walked away. Why had she

given him that odd look? As if she knew something he didn't but should. He shook his head. Women.

"Are the students settling in all right?"

Charles glanced down at Olivia's waiting smile. "They aren't going to settle in too well until the parents leave. A few are staying over for the picnic tomorrow but most are heading home today after dinner."

She nodded. "I'm looking forward to the picnic. We've been baking for several days."

"So has Selma. The whole place smells like peaches and cinnamon."

She laughed. "The children must love that."

"Hey, I love it, too. She's served peach cobbler for the past two days because she knows it's a favorite with the students and teachers."

Her laughter trilled pleasantly, and he grinned. He could make her laugh, too. "Did your mother tell you I dropped by one day last week when you were in town?"

"Yes. I'm sorry I missed you." She glanced up at him, her eyes sparkling.

Charles started. "I never noticed the color of your eyes before."

"Blue?" Confusion wrinkled her brow. "You've known me for years and never knew my eyes were blue?"

He laughed. "Of course I knew they were blue. But I just noticed they're more like deep sapphire. Almost the color of our pond back home. Very pretty."

A blush deepened the pink of her cheeks. "Thank you, Charles. That's a nice thing to say."

He cleared his throat. "I'd best help round up the boys. Selma won't like it if her dinner gets cold."

"Yes, I need to go, too. I'll see you at the picnic tomorrow."

"Maybe we can find a quiet place to eat so we can talk?" He wanted to get her opinion about Jeremiah.

"Yes, of course." Those beautiful sapphire eyes sparkled again.

"Good. I'll see you there."

He headed toward the wagon where the boys and some of the staff were already loaded up and waiting for him.

Trent Quincy stood by the wagon. "Charles. Good. I want to run something by you."

"Sure, Doc, what is it?"

"What would you think of adding a horseback riding class to the school curriculum?" He leaned against the wagon and pushed back his hat, a satisfied look on his face.

Dr. Quincy's grandmother had donated the mansion and land for a school for the deaf many years ago, after her own deaf child had died of an illness. She'd turned over the responsibility of establishing and running the school to her son, Trent's father. A few years ago, the ownership and responsibility for the school had passed into Trent's hands. Other than the medical needs of the students and staff, Trent left most decisions concerning the school in his director's hands. So Charles knew he would have checked with her first.

"What does P.H. think?"

"She thinks it's a great idea. But since you're the one in charge of the boys' outdoor activities, she said it should be your decision."

Charles thought for a moment. It would be extra work and time, but the benefit to the boys would be more than worth it.

"Where will we get the horses? The carriage horses won't do."

"As a matter of fact, I bought a couple last week. Didn't

really need them, but they were being mishandled so I made an offer and the owner grabbed it."

"You know, the care of two extra horses will be more work for Albert." Their stableman and all-around handyman was getting up in years.

"Already thought of that. The boys who want to take the class will have to agree to help Albert."

Charles nodded and grinned. Seemed the doc had thought of everything. "Bring them on over. I'll start signing boys up tomorrow."

Thank You, Lord. This could be just the thing to help Jeremiah. What boy can resist a horse?

Chapter 3

Olivia walked across the still-green lawn from the parsonage to the back of the church where the men had set up a number of tables. The churchyard bustled with people who'd been arriving in buggies and wagons since midmorning. The community was more than ready for a get-together and celebration after the long, busy summer. Of course, most of them were in the beginning stages of harvesting their crops and the women were already busy canning. But for this day, they would put aside their labors and have a good time.

Several women spread spotless white cloths on the tables. More than likely, they wouldn't be spotless for long. Squeals of laughter rent the air from the direction of the river. Apparently, some of the children were already having fun. The memory of wading in the cold river and being splashed by other children washed over her. She could almost feel the chill on her toes.

She set her heavy basket on a bench and began unloading jars of bread-and-butter pickles, okra pickles, peach preserves, condiments, napkins, plates and silverware onto one end of the table. Most families would bring their own table settings, but Mama always set out extra in case anyone forgot theirs. And someone always did. Not to mention the single men who never thought to bring anything but hungry appetites.

Abigail came around the corner of the building. Several girls converged on her and took the almost year-old baby girl, Celeste, from her arms. Olivia grinned. They'd be bringing her back soon enough when she needed a fresh diaper. Trent followed his wife with a huge basket in each hand. And Carrie, their cook and housekeeper, carried another.

"Trent, just set them on one of the tables. I'll have to sort things out." Abigail waved at Olivia. "I see you're already busy."

"I've hardly started yet. Something in your basket sure smells good."

"Carrie and I baked chicken with peaches. I figured there would be more than enough fried chicken to go around." Abigail bent over one of the baskets and started pulling out goodies.

"I love your peach-baked chicken. Mama does, too, but she never makes it because Pa doesn't care for it." Olivia picked up her basket. "I'd better get another load. See you later."

When she reached the kitchen, Mama was handing a full basket to Jake. "Now be careful. The pecan pies and my chocolate layer cake are in this one."

"Yes, ma'am," Jake said. "I sure wouldn't want anything to happen to that cake."

"Oh, go on with you." Mama waved him away and

turned to Olivia. "Both those covered platters are full of fried chicken. Why don't you put them in the small basket and carry them out? I'll fill up the other baskets."

"All right, Mama." Olivia reached for one of the platters. "Where's Father? I thought he'd help carry things."

Mama scurried back and forth from the cupboards to the kitchen table, her hands filled with food. She paused and laid the back of her hand against her forehead. "Oh, my. I forgot to tell you. Old Mrs. Waters is ill. Her grandson, Dewey, came and got your father. The poor old dear told Dewey over and over she was about to die and needed her pastor. Finally, he took her seriously."

"Oh, no. I hope she'll be all right." But she hated for Papa to miss the picnic. A twinge of guilt bit at her conscience when she realized she was being selfish.

"Well, dear. She's suffered for a long time. It would be merciful if the Lord would take her on home."

Olivia nodded and bit her lip, then finished loading her basket. As soon as she stepped out the door, three of the girls from the school came running over. Molly Flannigan and her friend Trudy took the basket from her.

"Well, thank you, girls. I could have carried it. But since you want to help, I'll go back and get more things to take over."

"No," the three girls chorused.

Olivia eyed them. Okay, maybe they weren't just being helpful. "Is something wrong?"

All three girls were totally deaf but excellent lip-readers, and although their speech was different, most of the time Olivia could easily understand them. But when they all began to talk at once, the noise totally obscured any semblance of understandable speech.

"Wait, wait." Olivia smiled. She made the sign for stop,

hitting her left palm with the edge of her right hand. "One at a time, please."

Pretty, blonde, blue-eyed Margaret Long, a little older than the other two girls, took a deep breath and placed both hands on her narrow hips. "It's like this, Miss Olivia. Did you know the school has started horseback riding classes?"

"No, I didn't." Puzzled, she let her gaze roam over each of their faces. "But that sounds like fun. What is wrong with that?"

"They're only letting the boys take the class." Trudy's eyes clouded over and a frown creased her brow. "Do you think that's fair? We want to ride, too."

"Oh. Well, did they give you a reason?" Olivia searched around in her mind for wisdom. "Did they think you girls might get hurt?"

"They didn't give us any reason." Molly stomped her small foot. "When we asked Mr. Charles if we could take the class, he just told us it is for boys only."

That sounded unfair to Olivia as well, but she didn't want to jump to conclusions and contribute to rebellion in the girls without talking to Charles first.

"I'll tell you what. I'll check into it and try to find out why. But I'm not making any promises. He may have a good reason for his decision." She tried to keep her expression composed. It wouldn't do for them to see that she was already taking their side. "So can you girls have a good time today and leave the matter to me?"

"Yes, ma'am," they each said in turn. Molly and Trudy headed toward the tables with the basket but Margaret remained standing there.

"Is there something else, Margaret?"

The girl took a deep breath. "If Mr. Charles thinks we'll get hurt, will you tell him I've been riding since I was seven?"

Olivia suppressed a smile. "Yes, I will tell him that."

Olivia shook her head and smiled as Margaret ran to join her friends, then she walked to the house to fetch another basket of food.

Soon, the makeshift tables groaned beneath the abundance of meats, desserts, side dishes and every kind of pickle and preserve imaginable. Women sent their husbands to the river to fetch the children.

"Here comes the reverend!" The shout was followed by applause, as Papa rode his horse to the barn.

Charles walked up to her. "Don't forget we're eating together."

Pleasure mixed with anxiety shot through her. She hated to ruin their time together by questioning his decision about the girls. But he probably had a good reason. And the girls would need to understand. "I haven't forgotten."

As soon as Papa announced that Mrs. Waters was only suffering from indigestion, relieved laughter and applause broke out. He then asked the blessing, and a line quickly formed beside the food-laden tables. Olivia and Charles filled their plates and settled beneath one of the massive live oaks surrounding the church.

Olivia smoothed her skirts around her, making sure her legs and ankles were covered. She sometimes wondered why women's clothing had to be so complicated.

Charles took a couple of bites of a drumstick and washed it down with a swallow of lemonade.

She'd wait until they finished eating to bring up the subject of the riding class.

Full from the delicious meal, Olivia began to grow drowsy. She jerked her head up and met Charles's amused gaze. She jumped up and began to gather their plates, silverware and napkins. "Let's walk along the river."

"Sounds good. Better not get too close, though, unless you want those ornery boys splashing you."

She laughed as they put away the dishes and things, then she tucked her hand in the crook of his arm. "They wouldn't dare splash their Sunday school teacher."

"I wouldn't be too sure. They soaked their English teacher last year." He laughed. "She was mad as a hornet."

"Oh, yes. I remember. Helen had to go back to the school and change." She took a deep breath and cut a glance at him. Did it still bother him that Helen had married Mr. Flannigan?

"Was that a sigh I heard?"

She shook her head. "No, not really, but I do have something I need to ask you about."

"Ask away." They'd reached the riverbank and he guided her along the path that had been pounded out by hundreds of footsteps over the year.

"Well." She hesitated. "I'm sure you have a perfectly good reason, but would you mind telling me why the girls are excluded from your riding class?"

He grinned and peered at her. "Oh. You're serious, aren't you?"

"Very serious. I simply want to know."

"And, excuse me for parroting some of your words, but the answer is perfectly simple. I can't teach girls to ride."

She stopped walking and frowned. "And why is that, I'd like to know?"

"There are several reasons, Livvy. Why does it matter to you?" He scratched his head and confusion filled his eyes.

"If you aren't going to include them, I think they have a right to know why." She peered into his eyes. "They think you're playing favorites. I'm sure they're wrong about that, but you need to give them a reason."

He frowned. "All right. One reason is that they don't

have the proper clothing. They can't ride in dresses. It wouldn't be modest."

Olivia's heart lightened. He did have a good explanation, but one she could fix. "That's easy to remedy. I'll ask some of the ladies to help me make riding skirts for them. We'll start right away."

Charles's face blanched and panic washed over it. "Wait, that's not the only reason. Girls have to ride sidesaddle. I wouldn't know the first thing about that. So, you see, they can't take the class."

"No problem. I'll teach them."

Surprise filled his eyes and he stared at her for a moment, groping around in his mind for another reason. When nothing came to him, he shook his head. "Fine. I accept your offer. I'm sure you'll be an excellent teacher."

Chapter 4

What had she been thinking to get herself into such a predicament? Olivia twisted the initialed handkerchief she'd received from one of her Sunday school students last Christmas. How could she have been so foolish as to say she'd teach horseback riding?

Abigail sat on the settee across from her in the Quincys' back parlor, a look of amusement on her face. "Just tell Charles you've changed your mind."

"I can't. I'd have to tell him the reason. That would be utterly humiliating." She bit her bottom lip and heaved a sigh. "Besides, I can't let the girls down. I'm sure he's told them by now."

"Hmm. Maybe you could put them off while you take a few lessons."

"It's not lessons I need, Abby. I learned to ride, at my father's insistence, when I was a child. But I never got over my fear of horses." A shudder ran through her body. "I don't know why. As long as they're hitched up to a buggy, they don't bother me at all. But when they get too close I freeze up, and the thought of mounting one again makes me sick to my stomach."

Concern crossed Abigail's face. "Oh, honey. You're serious, aren't you? I had no idea it was that bad."

Olivia nodded. She couldn't remember ever feeling so helpless.

"Okay, we have to make the riding dresses, so you have a little time to figure this out. And since most of the women are busy canning, it could take us a while to get them all done."

A moment of relief surged through Olivia, followed by another wave of despair. "But that doesn't solve my problem. Sooner or later I'll have to face it."

Abigail sat up straighter. "True. But in the meantime, you're going to overcome your fear."

"How?"

"Well, I don't know. But we'll think of something. I'd better see if Trent has an idea that might help."

"But what if he tells Charles?" The thought of Charles laughing at her predicament was more than she could bear.

"He won't. I'll make him promise not to tell anyone."

"Well, all right. But I don't see how I can possibly get over this fear I've had almost all my life."

"I know one thing you need to do." Abigail hesitated, then taking a deep breath, she continued, "Have you ever prayed about it?"

"A little. But mostly, I just stayed away from horses as much as possible." Truthfully, she'd seldom thought to pray about it. It hadn't seemed that important before.

"Maybe it's time for you to face your fear." At the sound of a sharp cry, Abigail jumped up. "My angel girl is awake. I'll be right back."

Olivia leaned back and closed her eyes. "Father, I know I need to get over this fear. But I can't do it myself. Please help me."

A moment later, Abigail returned, carrying her curly haired little girl. She sat and bounced the child on her knees. The child chortled with giggles. It must be wonderful to have such a sweet baby. Maybe someday. Olivia took a deep breath. But she had other things to think about now.

"Abby, you don't need to ask Trent. I know what I have to do."

Abigail tickled Celeste beneath her chubby baby chin, then cast a curious look in Olivia's direction. "Well, are you going to tell me?"

"It's simple. I have to spend time with our horses. I have to saddle and bridle and get myself into the saddle and ride. No matter how scared I am. And trust God. It's the only way."

"Good for you. Sometimes we simply have to take the bull by the horns and plunge into the storm."

Olivia giggled. "I think that's what they call a mixed metaphor."

Abigail looked blank for a moment then laughed. "Well, you know what I mean." She turned to the baby on her lap. "Auntie Olivia is making fun of your mama, sweetie."

Celeste patted her mother's lips.

Olivia laughed and stood. "I'd best be going. The horses have been hitched to the buggy long enough. I'd only meant to stop by for a moment."

"Do you want me to go with you when you face the challenge?" Abigail stood, shifting Celeste to her hip. "I don't mind."

Maybe that would make things easier. But, on second thought, maybe not. Olivia shook her head. "Thanks, but

I think I need to do this alone. Except maybe for Jake. Just in case."

"All right. Be careful. And let me know how it goes."

Olivia waved as she drove away. Why was she comfortable driving the carriage, but terrified at the thought of approaching a horse any other way? There must be a reason.

Lord, why am I so fearful? No one else seems to have a problem like mine. Please help me.

She drove around to the barn and pulled up by the sycamore tree. Jake came out to meet her with his friendly smile. He'd come to work for her father when she was only nine and was more of a friend than an employee. She started to climb down from the carriage, then stopped. "I'll drive them in, Jake. I want to help get them unharnessed."

He shot her a startled look. "Are you sure about this, Miss Olivia?"

"Yes, I am. But promise you won't tell anyone."

"You want me to lie?"

Olivia almost laughed at the horror in his voice. He'd no more think of lying to her father than he'd think of slapping him across the face.

"No, of course not. But you don't have to mention it, do you? That's not lying."

"Well, I don't know. Don't like keeping things from your pa."

"Well, goodness, it's not as if I'm doing something wrong, is it?"

He grinned. "I reckon not. All right, guess I won't spill the beans. I'm glad you decided to tackle your fears."

Heaven's sake! How many other people knew she was afraid of horses?

Charles banged on the director's oak door. What in tarnation was taking her so long?

"I'm coming! Don't beat the door down." P.H. flung it open, her glare boring through Charles's skull. "What is it?"

"I need to talk to you about something important, if you have time."

She stood aside. "All right. Come in." She sat down in her desk chair, and waved him to the seat across from her. One blond curl escaped the severe bun on the back of her head, belying her fifty-some-odd years. Her eyes softened into their usual kind expression. "Obviously, something has you in a dither. What's wrong?"

He leaned forward. "Olivia Shepherd has this fool idea that the girl students should be included in the riding class."

A glimmer of interest brightened the director's blue eyes. "Really? That's a wonderful idea." She peered at him intently. "Obviously, you don't think so. Why not?"

He snorted. "She thinks she's going to teach them."

Surprise filled her eyes. "Well, that *is* interesting. And why does she think she's more qualified than you?"

He sighed. "Well, to be honest, it wasn't exactly that way."

"I suggest, to save time and to prevent me from kicking you out of my office, you tell me what way it was. Start from the beginning and don't hem and haw around."

Charles fought a grin. No one could accuse P.H. Wellington of being subtle. He took a deep breath and told her the story from beginning to end.

Amusement danced in her eyes when he'd finished. "Serves you right."

"I know, but you'll help me get out of it, won't you? Tell her it's not a good idea?" He threw her a hopeful look.

"Absolutely not. I think it's a fine idea." She scooted her chair out and stood. "So do what you need to do to implement this. I'll leave the scheduling up to you, since you're in charge of the program."

The next thing Charles knew he was standing in the hall outside her closed door. A growl threatened to explode from his throat. That surely didn't go the way he'd planned. Why were women so stubborn and opinionated? Especially Livvy and P.H.

He slammed through the front porch and leaned against one of the pillars. Laughter drifted his way from the direction of the orchard. He sauntered over, the smell of peaches tantalizing his taste buds. Albert and some of the older boys were harvesting the last of the crop, while the younger ones picked up fruit that had fallen to the ground. Cook would look through those carefully and salvage the good ones for peach butter. The thought made Charles's mouth water.

Jeremiah waved from one of the top branches, a grin splitting his face. The sight was encouraging. The boy was good-natured when he wasn't being mean to the younger boys.

Charles returned the wave and walked around the house to the old stable to see how the work was going. It hadn't been used for years since the carriage horses and mules had been housed in the barn. But with the addition of the new horses, Trent had hired a couple of men to repair the stable. Charles grinned. He wouldn't put it past his friend to fill the building with horses.

He grunted. Then sighed. Maybe he was making too much of this. But he'd seen Livvy shy away from horses before and suspected that she was afraid of them. He also suspected that she'd spoken before she thought. There was only one thing to do, since P.H. was being obstinate. He'd talk to Trent and see if he'd go over the director's head and put a stop to the whole thing.

An hour later, when Trent dismounted and tied his horse, Warrior, to the hitching rail beside the porch, Charles clapped his friend on the shoulder. "Have a minute to talk before you check on the students?"

"Sure, is something wrong? No new illnesses, I hope."

Charles shook his head. Trent was devoted to the children of Quincy School and their health was one of his main concerns. During a measles epidemic the year before, the doctor had remained at the school night and day until all risks were past. Charles was happy not to have bad news for him. "No. Just a little matter I need to discuss with you."

"What can I help with, Charles?"

Charles cleared his throat. Maybe he shouldn't put Trent on the spot like this. He took a deep breath. He might as well go ahead. "I guess you know that Olivia wants to teach the girls to ride horseback."

Trent peered at him, his eyes questioning. "Uh-huh. Abigail is going to help make riding habits. Why?"

"I don't think it's a good idea." Now that was an intelligent answer. His face warmed at the amusement in Trent's eyes and Charles frowned. What was so funny about it? "I mean, after all, she's not a teacher."

"Sure, she is. She teaches Sunday school. Has for years."

Charles snorted. "Well, that's a far cry from teaching a child to ride a horse."

"What does P.H. think about the idea?"

"She's taking Olivia's side, of course. You know how women stick together."

"I also know P.H. wouldn't agree to it unless she felt it was a good idea. So unless you have a better reason than the one you've given, I'm not about to go over her head."

Charles's stomach clenched. Should he tell Trent of his concern about Livvy's fear? But that wouldn't be fair. Especially since he wasn't one hundred percent sure about it. Besides, Trent wasn't likely to go against his wife and the director without a good reason.

"Tell you what, Charles." Trent slapped him on the shoulder. "Let's give it a try. If things aren't going well, I'll talk to P.H. and maybe we'll cancel the class." He held out his hand.

Feeling like an idiot for bringing the matter up to Trent in the first place, he shook his friend's hand then followed him into the house where delicious aromas wafted up the hall from the kitchen. Fine. A trial period it would be. But Charles planned to keep a close eye on Livvy to make sure she didn't get spooked and cause herself or one of the students to get hurt.

Or maybe he could convince her to give up the idea. After all, he was doing this for her own good.

Chapter 5

The road to the school veered to the left. Livvy straightened and took a deep breath as she turned onto the narrow lane. She could do this. After all, she'd be fitting the girls for their new riding dresses and wouldn't be anywhere near the horses today. So why were the muscles in her back and chest tighter than her corset, and why was she clenching the reins so tightly she could barely feel her fingers?

Forcing herself to relax, Livvy blotted her forehead with her handkerchief and inhaled deeply. The scent of still-blooming honeysuckle drifted past and she glanced around. The vines with their golden-throated blooms sprawled over the wire fence beside the road. Oak and pecan trees stood sentinel over the lane, interspersed with the occasional sweet gum.

A wooden gate loomed ahead, with a hanging sign to the side that proclaimed Cecilia Quincy School for the Deaf. A tiny magnolia tree reached upward as though trying to reach the height of the one destroyed by last year's tornado. Livvy reined the horses in, but before she could get down from the buggy, a grinning Albert appeared and swung the gate open for her.

"Afternoon, Miss 'Livia," his melodic voice sang out, causing an unexplainable thrill of joy to course through her.

"Good afternoon, Albert. How do you always know when someone is at the gate?"

He scratched his grizzly head. "Well, now, I don't rightly know, Miss 'Livia. You reckon I's a prophet?" A loud guffaw exploded from his lips. "Naw, I think it's because Miz Wellington tol' me you was coming and to be on the lookout."

Livvy laughed and waved as she drove through the gate. The lane curved past a magnolia tree, and the white-frame, three-story building that housed the school came into view. Lush green lawns spread across the front of the house and surrounded it. Farther back, thick woods created the perfect backdrop to the beautiful picture.

Livvy drove around to the barn and stepped out of the buggy. Michael, one of the older students, gave her a shy grin and took the reins.

She found Virgie inside the front door, waiting. Did everyone at Quincy know she was coming today?

"Miss Olivia, you go on into the parlor and have a cup of tea with Miz Flannigan. Classes will be dismissed soon." Her soft drawl fell pleasantly on Livvy's ears.

She thanked Virgie, then went into the small parlor where she found Helen sitting on the settee with a steaming cup of tea in her hand.

"Helen, I'm so glad to see you."

Helen scooted over and patted the cushion beside her. "To be honest, I forgot this was the day you were fitting the girls. But I'm glad I came early. This will give us a chance to catch up."

Livvy poured herself a cup of tea from the rose-and-white teapot on the table then tossed a suspicious glance at the other woman. What exactly did she mean to catch up on?

Helen didn't keep her waiting long. "I hear that Charles isn't too thrilled about your teaching the girls to ride."

"No, he isn't completely happy with the idea."

"Well, I think it's wonderful. Molly lived in the city before she came to live with us and I don't suppose it crossed anyone's mind to teach her to ride."

"No, I don't suppose it would have, living in town." She frowned. Where was this leading?

"Well, it's high time someone did and I applaud you." Helen set her cup down on a side table. "I'd love to help sew the girls' riding costumes."

Relief coursed through Livvy. She should be ashamed of herself for thinking Helen had wanted to tear into Charles. Or perhaps gloat because he was upset with Livvy. When would she get over her attitude toward Helen?

"Thank you. We can always use another pair of hands. I'd like to get the classes started before the winter rains set in."

"When's your first meeting?"

"Tomorrow morning. Saturday was the only time we could get everyone together. We'll cut out patterns and decide who will do what. Of course, some of us will have more time to devote to the project than others. But there will be plenty of work to go around. We have seven ladies who've volunteered so far, including you."

A tap at the door drew their attention. Livvy bit her lip as she counted five girls in the doorway. She had thought there would be three at the most. Oh, dear.

Molly grinned at her mother then turned to Livvy. "Miss Olivia, we'll be waiting upstairs in the sewing room whenever you're ready for us."

"I'll go with you now." She stood.

"Can you use some help?" asked Helen.

"I certainly can. Abigail had planned to come with me, but Carrie was busy canning, so there was no one to watch the baby."

With glowing faces, the girls led the way up two flights of stairs and down the west hall, chattering and laughing, then stepped aside to let the women precede them into the recently converted sewing room.

Trudy sauntered over to Livvy and took her hand. "Miss Olivia, thank you so much for getting us into the class."

"It was my pleasure." She glanced around at the girls. "Let's see now. Elizabeth, you're twelve, aren't you?"

"Yes, ma'am." Elizabeth opened her brown eyes wide. "I'll be thirteen next month. That's not too old for the class, is it?"

"Of course not. I just like to know everyone's ages."

Molly stepped forward. "Trudy and I are both eleven, Miss Olivia."

"Thank you, Molly."

"I'm almost thirteen, too," Margaret offered.

Livvy nodded at the girl who had caused such a stir last year. But now the blonde, blue-eyed beauty was sweet as could be, most of the time.

With a sigh, Livvy turned to Lily Ann, who stood with a look of dread on her face, her lovely, but sightless, chocolate-brown eyes staring straight ahead. She wasn't volunteering anything. "Lily Ann?"

The girl swallowed. "I'm nine. But I can learn to ride. I know I can."

Sympathy tugged at Livvy's heart.

"Honey, I believe you. And I'm going to go ahead and measure you for a riding outfit. But I'll have to talk to Miss Wellington before I can accept you into the class."

She swallowed. "Yes, ma'am."

An hour later, after measuring, marking, pinning and writing down measurements, Livvy said goodbye, promising to come again next week to talk about the class.

Her heart jumped at the sight of Charles standing on the front porch. He pushed away from the pillar and smiled. "I see you survived."

Attraction turned to irritation, and she glared. "Why wouldn't I? They're wonderful girls."

"Of course. I know they are. I didn't mean to imply that they weren't."

Mollified, she nodded. "Oh. All right."

"I was actually waiting here to ask you to have lunch with me at the hotel tomorrow."

Pleasure washed over her. "Yes, I'd love to."

"How about I pick you up at eleven? We can go for a drive first."

Livvy's heart danced and she couldn't keep the big smile from her face. "Yes, that would be…" She stopped. "Oh. I can't go that early. I'm meeting with the ladies about the riding habits. We won't be finished before noon."

"That's no problem. They serve lunch until two on Saturday. How does twelve-thirty sound? We'll go eat lunch then take our drive."

"That's fine, Charles. See you then."

She hummed all the way home. Charles wasn't upset with her after all.

Silverware gleamed on the white tablecloths and waiters bustled throughout the room, napkins over their arms and trays lifted high.

Charles smiled across the table at Livvy as she lifted her napkin and gave her lips a dainty pat.

A waiter appeared at their table and began removing dishes. He nodded at Charles. "I'll be right back to refill your coffee and take your dessert orders."

"Oh, heavens." Livvy gave a slight laugh. "Nothing for me. I couldn't eat another bite."

"Me, either. But we'll take those refills, if you please."

"Yes, sir." The waiter headed toward the kitchen with the laden tray.

Charles leaned back and sighed. "Their desserts are good, but they can't hold a candle to your mother's."

"Very true. But Mother doesn't make ice cream."

"Oh. Would you like some?"

"No, I'm much too full. The meal was delicious." She sent him a sweet smile.

Charles hoped she'd still be smiling when he said what he intended to say. But someone had to reason with her.

"Goodness, Charles. What a serious expression. I'd almost think you were glaring at me."

"Oh…sorry." He straightened and cleared his throat. "Actually, I'd like to talk to you about something."

"Well, go ahead. Talk away." She waved her hand toward him and grinned.

He picked up his teaspoon and began tapping it against his cup as he exhaled the breath he hadn't noticed he'd been holding. "Livvy, I really wish you'd reconsider about teaching the girls to ride."

Surprise crossed her face. And something else. Disappointment? His stomach sank.

"I thought we had this settled. You have a new reason now?" She shot the words like rifle bullets.

"I don't think it's safe." Well, that sounded rather pathetic. He should have thought this out a little better.

"Why is it safe for the boys and unsafe for the girls?"

Irritation bit at him. "Well, that's obvious, isn't it? The boys are bigger and stronger."

"Really? Sonny is bigger and stronger than Elizabeth and Margaret?"

"You know what I mean, Livvy. Don't be unreasonable."

"Unreasonable? I'm being unreasonable?" She stood. "I'm not the one thinking up ridiculous excuses to make a point. I'm surprised at you, Charles. And very disappointed. Now please stop banging that spoon before you break the cup. And take me home."

He stood, and glanced around, relieved that the few people who remained in the dining room were focused on their meals. He motioned for the waiter to bring their bill.

When they were in the buggy, he turned to Olivia. "Please don't be angry, Livvy. If you'd think it over, you'd see that I'm right."

"No. You're being unfair to the girls again and I won't stand for it. P.H. gave me permission and I won't back down and disappoint those girls."

He sighed. Should he tell her he knew about her fear of horses? That this was the reason he kept trying to stop her from continuing? But, no, if she wanted him to know, she'd have told him. He'd just have to do what he could to help.

The buggy wheels rolled through the wooded area and they came out in a clearing. If only he could clear away the past hour and not bring up the subject of the riding class at all. All he'd done was make Livvy mad.

Funny how her anger affected him. He'd seen her mad plenty of times and merely laughed it off. But this was different. She hadn't said a word since they'd left Magnolia Junction and she radiated pain. Somehow, he'd hurt her. He didn't know how, but this was about something more than horseback riding lessons.

* * *

So much for Charles wanting her company. He'd only wanted to convince her to back out of teaching the girls to ride. And that she would not do. Pain ripped through her. She might as well face it. Charles Waverly would never have the feelings for her that she did for him. And right now she wasn't even sure he wanted to be her friend.

Chapter 6

By the time Charles drove the buggy into the barn, the knot in his stomach was tighter than ever. He allowed his mind to wander back and forth over the afternoon in an attempt to decide what had made Livvy so mad. They'd had the same conversation before, sort of. And she was irritated. But to get so mad that she just hopped out of the buggy on her own and didn't even say goodbye?

He had to clear his mind. He'd promised the boys to take them riding before dark.

But why was she so upset?

The boys came running out the back door.

"Mr. Charles!" The younger ones were almost bouncing in their excitement. He broke them into two groups and instructed one group to help Albert in the stable while he took the other four for a short ride.

The ride down a familiar and well-traveled path started out pleasantly and uneventfully, and the boys' excited chatter was almost enough to keep Charles's mind off Olivia.

Then a scream rent the air and Jimmy slid to one side of his saddle, waving frantically, his eyes wide with fear.

Charles jumped off his horse and hurried to shove the youngster upright.

Jimmy grabbed Charles's arm and held on, his small body trembling. "A cougar! I saw a cougar!"

Charles scanned the area, seeing nothing resembling a cougar or even a bobcat. "Where did you see it, Jimmy?"

Jimmy pointed a shaking finger toward the woods to their right. "Over there."

"There's nothing there now, Jimmy, and cougars don't usually come out in the daytime."

"But I saw it, Mr. Charles."

The boy had likely spotted a large barn cat or some farmer's hog, but Charles didn't want to embarrass the child. "Well, whatever you saw is gone now. Let's turn around and head back. The other boys are waiting their turn."

By the time they got back to the barn, Jimmy had calmed down a little. But as soon as his feet hit the dirt, he ran to the other boys and told them about the cougar. His audience listened with bated breath and wide eyes. Charles grinned and shook his head.

"All right, boys, it's your turn to work in the stable. The rest of you adjust your stirrups for your ride and check the cinches well."

They hurried to comply, but continued to talk excitedly about the cougar Jimmy thought he had seen. All except Jeremiah, who threw them all a disgusted look and headed for his horse to check the stirrups.

Charles watched carefully as the boy tightened the cinch, and then loosened it slightly. "Good job, Jeremiah."

He'd seen Jeremiah help saddle one of the horses earlier. Whoever had taught him had done a thorough job.

Jeremiah nodded slightly. "Can I mount?" Amazing how clearly he could speak when he wanted to.

"Yes, but keep him steady and wait for the rest of us."

This trip would include Charles, Jeremiah, Sonny and Tommy. Taking Jeremiah out with the two younger boys was risky. Charles had seen more signs of bullying lately, but he couldn't prove anything. He'd just have to keep an eye on them all.

"Now, we're going to start slowly since this is the first time you've handled the reins yourselves. And be sure to do everything I tell you."

"Okay, Mr. Charles."

"Okay, Mr. Charles."

As Jeremiah snorted and shook his head, an idea crossed Charles's mind. "Listen, Sonny and Tommy. Jeremiah's an experienced rider, so pay attention to him, too."

Trepidation hit him. What was he thinking? Their tormentor might be capable of deliberately leading them astray.

A look of surprise crossed Jeremiah's face, then he tightened his lips and turned his head. He cleared his throat. "Yes, I've been riding for years. I guess it's okay if they watch me."

Charles dipped his head to hide a grin. The boy had deliberately turned so the younger ones couldn't read his lips. Apparently, he didn't want to show any signs of softening to them.

To be on the safe side, Charles took a different trail this time, with Jeremiah in the lead and Charles bringing up the rear. He was pleased to see that the older boy was on good behavior, and when they stopped by a creek to stretch their legs, Jeremiah even helped Sonny remount properly and then checked the cinches.

In spite of Sonny and Tommy craning their necks to see into the woods, no cougar was spotted and the ride was uneventful, except for their sighs of disappointment.

Charles was amused when Sonny signed to Tommy, "Maybe we'll see a cougar next time."

"Yeah," Tommy signed back. "Or maybe at least an armadillo or something."

Dusk was starting to fall when they arrived back in the barn. After taking care of the horses, they headed for the house.

"That's fried chicken I smell." Sonny took off running, followed closely by his friends. The two older boys weren't far behind.

They all washed up and headed for the dining room, where the other children and staff were already seated at the table.

Charles slipped into his chair next to Howard, the boys' dorm supervisor. They'd no sooner said grace than the serving girls entered. The tantalizing aroma of shrimp and tomato bisque made Charles realize how hungry he was.

The delicious food, as well as the conversation and friendly banter among P.H. and the teachers, made for an enjoyable dinner experience. But when Charles entered his room later, the thoughts he'd held at bay since he arrived back at the school from his time with Livvy came roaring back and, with them, questions and accusations. He must have done something besides asking her not to give the girls riding lessons. But for the life of him, he couldn't figure it out.

Well, he'd see her at church the next day. Maybe he should ask her outright. After all, he wasn't a mind reader. He was probably exaggerating the situation in his mind anyway. Yes, that was it. When he saw her tomorrow, she'd be her usual, friendly self and invite him to Sunday dinner. Maybe Mrs. Shepherd would make one of her delicious apple pies. He wouldn't dare tell Cook, but he was getting a little tired of peach. With the matter settled in his mind, he punched his pillow a few times then yawned and closed his eyes. All was well.

Livvy settled herself onto the piano bench, smoothing her new skirt across her knees. She'd chosen the cranberry-colored fabric with a print of tan leaves because it reminded her of fall, her favorite season. She fanned herself with her hand. Lord knew it seemed to be taking its time coming to Georgia this year. Adjusting the brand-new hymnal, she glanced toward the door. She'd hoped Charles would be there before she had to seat herself at the piano so she could snub him right away, but so far the Quincy School group hadn't arrived.

A hand touched her shoulder, and she smiled up into her father's sparkling eyes.

"I see you're ready to worship our Lord this morning, daughter."

Guilt rippled through her, but she managed to nod and widen her smile as he stepped away. Had she even thought of worship this morning? She turned as the door opened and two rows of children from the school walked down the aisle with Charles and the rest of the school staff close behind.

Quickly she faced forward and began to turn pages in the songbook. A glance from the corner of her eyes revealed the object of her ire scooting into the pew next to Jeremiah. Then he looked straight at Livvy. Humph. She'd show him just how important he was to her. He wouldn't get so much as another glance from her the rest of the morning.

Harley Johnson stepped up onto the platform and opened a songbook. "Good morning, brothers and sisters in the Lord."

Please, God, have him choose a song I know. There were several in the new book that had been recently published.

"Good morning," the congregation chorused.

Harley grinned. "Now if you'll open your hymnals to page 148, we'll sing 'Standing on the Promises of God.' First and second verses, then stand for the fourth." With that he lifted his hand and began.

By the end of the third song, perspiration beaded Livvy's brow and, with relief, she went to sit beside her mother, while her father stepped to the podium.

"The scripture for today's sermon is Ephesians 4:32."

With a sharp nod of her head, Livvy pressed her lips into a tight smile. This verse was about kindness. Hopefully, Mr. Charles Waverly would listen carefully and take it to heart.

"It says, 'And be ye kind one to another, tenderhearted, forgiving one another, even as God for Christ's sake hath forgiven you.'"

Livvy's head jerked up and shock surged through her. She'd forgotten the part about forgiveness. Was that God speaking to her? But Charles had been thoughtless. He'd gotten her hopes up and then dashed them to the ground.

But had he really? He didn't know how Livvy felt about him. He looked on her as a good friend, nothing more. *But, God, even a friend deserves to be treated kindly.*

Livvy groaned. Charles had never been intentionally unkind to her. She was the one who misunderstood. Sure, he wanted to talk her out of the riding classes, but that didn't mean he hadn't wanted to spend time with her, as well. She swallowed and took a deep breath. But she wasn't ready to spend any time in conversation with him. She wouldn't be rude, but she would make her excuses and go home. It still hurt too much. She couldn't even apologize for her actions the day before, because he'd want to know why.

Her thoughts continued to wander until a gentle nudge from her mother's elbow brought Livvy back from her daydreams. Mama gestured with her head and Livvy met her father's frown. Oh, dear. The message was over and she hadn't heard a word of the sermon after the Bible verse. She jumped up and headed for the piano.

After her father gave the invitation, then prayed, Livvy went around the sanctuary, gathering up hymnbooks and placing them in their racks. Maybe she could avoid seeing Charles at all today. When the last book was placed neatly away, she grabbed a dusting cloth from the back room and started wiping down the pews.

"Livvy, what on earth are you doing?" Mama stood with her hands on her hips, a worried look in her eyes.

"Just cleaning up a little before we leave."

"You know very well we clean the building thoroughly on Thursday and Monday. Now come along and help me get dinner on the table. Will you be inviting Charles?"

"Not today, Mama. I want to rest after dinner. Maybe read for a while."

"Oh—well, then." Mama reached out a hand and touched Livvy's forehead. "I hope you aren't coming down with something. You aren't acting like yourself at all."

"I'm fine, Mama. I assure you."

Resigned to probably seeing Charles, after all, she followed her mother out the front door. As she'd feared, he waited by the steps.

His eyes brightened when he saw her and he stepped forward. "Livvy, I thought I'd missed you."

She smiled. "Hello, Charles. It's nice to see you."

Confusion clouded his eyes. "Are you upset with me about the riding lessons?"

"Not at all." She might as well get it over with. "Actually, I'd like to apologize for my behavior yesterday."

"Well, all right. I guess I shouldn't have asked you to drop the class after P.H. approved it. But did I do something else to offend you?"

His brown eyes crinkled with concern and her heart did a flip inside her chest.

"You didn't do anything, Charles. I must have been having a bad day." She smiled. After all, he hadn't knowingly done anything. "Now I need to help Mama with dinner. Have a nice day."

She hurried away, but when she reached the parsonage, she glanced back to see him still gazing after her. She swallowed. She should probably go back and invite him to dinner. They could go for a drive or a walk. After all, they'd always been friends. But that wasn't enough anymore. It was time to draw away from him before her heart was completely shattered.

Chapter 7

Clad in her new deep red riding habit, Livvy leaned against the corral rail next to Abigail and watched the pretty bay mare nudge Trent's vest. When he held out a piece of apple, she nibbled it daintily.

"She's so pretty." Livvy sighed and pushed down the nervousness already settling in her stomach.

"Yes, and all ready for you, sidesaddle and all."

"I do appreciate you and Trent going to all this trouble for me."

"Nonsense. It's the only way I know to help you over your fear. And it's no trouble at all. After all, you'll be doing the school a service by teaching the girls how to ride. Heaven knows, I don't have the time."

Trent led the mare out through the gate and over to the mounting block. Olivia took a reluctant step in his direction.

Abigail took her arm and urged her forward. "Come on now, Livvy. You can do this."

Straightening her back and lifting her chin, Livvy stepped to the block. "Of course I can."

She placed her foot in one of the stirrups and took a deep breath. A moment later she was settled on the saddle, her right thigh secure between the pommels and her leg wrapped around the left horn, her skirt smooth across her legs. She glanced toward the ground and a wave of dizziness washed over her. Quickly, she closed her eyes.

"Are you sure you want to do this?"

Trent's voice brought her back with a jolt, and she opened her eyes. "I'm fine. It's just that I haven't been up this high in a while."

He gave her an encouraging smile and handed her the reins. "Take it slowly at first. Sugar is easy to handle, and I'll be beside you on Midnight." He mounted his horse and gave her a look of encouragement.

With her lips in a tight smile, she nodded. They started at a gentle walk down the lane.

Livvy sat naturally, with her back straight, but tension tightened her muscles. After a while, Sugar's gentle sway soothed her, and she forced her icy hands to relax.

Midnight edged closer to her mount, and a cold sweat broke out on her brow. Her breath sped up and she forced herself to inhale and exhale slowly.

The lane swerved into a lush green valley, and Sugar increased her speed to follow Midnight with no urging at all from Livvy. Soon they settled into a slow trot up and down soft, gentle slopes.

Finally, they rode back to the corral and Trent assisted her in dismounting. Relief surged through her as her riding boots touched the ground. A wave of dizziness washed over her and she grabbed Trent's arm.

"Are you all right?" Trent led her over to a bench beneath a sweet gum tree.

As she sank onto the bench, Abigail came running from the house. "Livvy, are you all right?"

"Fine. I'm fine. Just a little light-headed is all."

"Come to the house and have a glass of cold lemonade. Or maybe you'd rather have tea?"

"Either will be fine." She stood, forcing herself not to wobble.

"Trent, take her arm and help her to the house."

"No, no, don't fuss. I can walk fine on my own."

"Here, let me help." Trent took her elbow in his comforting hand. "I have to go to the house anyway to get my medical bag. I'm making rounds today to see some of my homebound patients."

By the time they reached the cozy parlor, Livvy felt much better. She sank into an overstuffed chair and Abigail sat on a matching one and picked up a small bell from the table between them.

Carrie came in response to the tinkle of the bell and Abigail asked her to bring tea and sandwiches. When the housekeeper left the room, Abigail turned to Livvy. A frown creased her brow and worry filled her eyes.

Livvy glanced away to avoid her friend's searching eyes.

"Your fear goes deeper than you led me to believe, doesn't it?"

With a sigh, she nodded. "Yes."

"Look. I can't tell you what to do, but I really think you need to reconsider teaching this class. Tell Charles and P.H. the truth. Maybe they'll find someone else."

"And if they don't? Then I've let the girls down. And I can't—" She paused as Carrie came into the parlor with the tea tray.

"Thanks, Carrie," Abigail said. "Don't bother with pouring. I'll take care of it. Is my angel still sleeping?"

"Yes, ma'am. Sleeping like a log. I just now checked on her."

"If she should awaken, will you watch her for a little while? Miss Olivia and I have things to discuss."

"You know I will. Watching that baby is what I love best." A broad smile stretched across her dark face and she left the room.

Abigail grinned. "I don't know what I'd do without Carrie."

"She's been working for Trent for a long time, hasn't she?"

"Yes. Her husband, Solomon, even longer. You know, when they were children, the three of them were best friends. They used to scandalize the county."

"Really? I didn't know that. Can't imagine Trent scandalizing anyone."

"Well, the main scandal was that they were friends. No one seemed to think anything about it when they were small, but when they got a little older, a lot of folks thought it wasn't right for Trent to spend so much time with them. You know the prejudice around here. Well, it was a lot worse twenty or thirty years ago." She tossed back a curl that had come loose. "But Trent didn't care. He loved them like his own brother and sister. Still does."

"Were they slaves?"

"No, but both sets of parents were until Trent's grandfather died. Mrs. Quincy was from the North and the first thing she did was to free all the slaves and give them land if they wanted to stay. Some left, but most of them are still around here, working their farms."

"So, did Solomon's family have a farm?"

"Yes, but it went to his older brother. Anyway, by that time, Trent had inherited all the Quincy property. He asked Solomon to come manage it for him, so he could concentrate on his medical practice and the school." She peered at Livvy. "But, let's get back to the subject at hand."

A clap of thunder reverberated through the room. Livvy jumped up. Reprieve.

"I'd better get home. I wouldn't want to get caught in a downpour."

Halfway home, the rain started. First tiny drops, then, as Mama would say, it was raining like cats and dogs. Livvy grinned. Whatever that meant.

Well, she'd done it. She'd managed a ride without totally disgracing herself. That was good. Because she intended to invite Charles to dinner on Sunday. She'd always made excuses when he suggested going for a ride. But this time, she'd invite him. Wouldn't he be surprised to see how well she could sit a horse. Perhaps, then, he'd realize she could perfectly well teach the girls to ride. He'd never know that she was quaking inside.

Rain fell in torrents with thunder and lightning that didn't appear close to letting up. Charles sighed as he looked out the window at the gloomy afternoon. When the storms had started two days ago, the children's excitement had tickled him and he also welcomed the rain, but now restlessness had settled over the students and teachers alike. At least mornings and early afternoons kept them busy in class. But even the lamps couldn't lighten the gloom.

Oh, well, it would stop when it stopped. He returned to the bookcase where he'd been shelving textbooks, and finished lining up the science section. That was it for the day. He'd like to hole up a little longer, but that would hardly be fair to the rest of the staff who were trying to keep the students occupied. After all, the boys usually had their riding lessons this time of day. In fact, all the students were accustomed to outside activities after school, and this was the second day in a row they'd been cooped up inside.

To be honest, the main thing bothering him was that he hadn't seen Livvy for a few days, since they couldn't take the kids to midweek services at church.

He headed down the hall to the former ballroom, which had been converted to an auditorium and activities room.

To his surprise, he found Helen and Hannah Wilson, the sign-language teacher, hauling boxes from the large closet at the back of the room. Whatever they were doing, the girls were excited about it, but the boys hung around in small groups, muttering and frowning.

Charles sauntered over to where Jeremiah and two other boys had their heads together.

"What's going on, fellows?"

All three boys jerked around, guilt on their faces. Jeremiah recovered quickly and threw Charles a cocky grin. "Just trying to think of something to do so we won't have to work on stupid fall decorations."

"I heard that, young man." Helen waltzed over and gave Jeremiah a mock frown, then repeated her words so he could read her lips. "You won't think it's stupid when you're having fun at the Harvest Festival."

Roger Brumley, a new student, scowled. "But it's girls' work."

Uh-oh. Time to step in before the boys got themselves in trouble. "Helen, do you really need the boys' help with this project?"

She tapped her foot and gazed at the boys' hopeful faces. "Oh, if you have another way to keep them busy, we can manage without them."

"I thought we could head out to the barn and stable and see if Albert has something we can do."

With wild cheers ringing in his ears, Charles gathered

up the younger boys and told them all to get into boots and rain gear.

They trudged across the lawn, wet mud squishing around their boots, and through the muddy barnyard. The smell of damp straw and manure drifted out through the open barn door. Albert was busy polishing a saddle.

"Need some help, Albert?" He walked over to the old man with the boys trailing behind.

Albert's eyes gleamed. "Ain't too much work to do today, but we can find something. I'se sure glad for the company." He glanced toward the back of the barn. "Some of them empty stalls need to be mucked out. Now that the horses are in the stable, I reckon Dr. Trent done say he goin' to buy some more cows. He keeps it up, we goin' have us a dairy farm."

Charles laughed. "Well, I doubt he's going that far. The school is growing pretty fast. I'm sure Dr. Trent wants to make sure there is plenty of milk and beef."

"If you say so." Albert grinned and stood up from the stool, hefting the heavy saddle onto one of the sawhorses by the wall.

A cry from the back of the barn sent Charles rushing to see what was wrong. Sonny lay on the straw-covered floor of one of the stalls. Blood trickled down from a cut and a knot was already forming on his head.

Charles knelt beside him. "What happened?"

Sonny swallowed, his face twisted with pain. "I tripped and fell."

Bobby frowned and shook his finger at Jeremiah. "You tripped him, Jeremiah."

Disappointment hit Charles hard. "Jeremiah, I thought we were past this type of behavior."

"I didn't trip him. Bobby's lying. Or maybe he just thought he saw me trip Sonny."

"Sonny? Did Jeremiah trip you?"

Sonny wrinkled his brow and peered at Jeremiah then back at Charles. "I don't know. I tripped. But I don't know if it was his foot or something else."

Charles sighed. It was Bobby's word against Jeremiah's. He cast a glance in Jeremiah's direction. Was that shame on his face? If the boy was guilty, Charles certainly hoped it was shame.

He helped Sonny up. "Let's get you inside and cleaned up."

"Do we all have to go in?"

"Yes, Jeremiah. I'm sorry to say I don't know whom to trust or whom to believe. But I can't take a chance on another one of the younger children being hurt."

With dragging feet and unusual silence, the boys trooped behind Charles back to the house.

Just when he'd thought Jeremiah was making progress, it seemed he'd reverted to cruelty again. Would they have to send the boy home? *God, I've seen the good in Jeremiah. I know You want me to help him. Please show me how.*

Chapter 8

Excitement surged through the school on Sunday morning, as clear skies and warm sun meant that students and staff could go to church. After being cooped up for several days, the girls were eager to attend Sunday school. The boys were ready for fresh air and exercise.

"Umm, I smell ham and eggs." Sonny rubbed his stomach and grinned up at Charles as he entered the dining room.

Charles grinned in agreement. The delicious aroma of coffee, ham, eggs and grits drifted through the building, and children and teachers alike marched into the dining room with an almost holiday air.

Afterward, Charles helped get everyone settled into the wagons, except for the ladies, who followed in the carriage.

Oak trees sported new, spreading canopies of gold- and orange-tipped leaves as they stood next to their green, live-oak sisters. Charles breathed in deeply of the slightly crisp air. In a couple of weeks, the fall colors would be predominant.

Buggies and wagons lined the churchyard. Charles, thankful for the kindness of the neighbors who always left space for the school wagons to park, pulled the one he was driving beneath one of two oak trees that stood together.

He set the brake and jumped down. As he helped the girls from the wagon, a flash of blue caught his eye. Olivia waved as she crossed the yard from the parsonage. Instead of going in through the side door of the church, she walked toward him with a smile.

Relief washed over Charles like a soft wind. Livvy was herself again.

He met her near the steps, laughter spilling up from his heart. "You look very beautiful this morning."

"Thank you, kind sir." She flashed a grin and the blue of her eyes sparkled. "I see you all survived the storms."

"We survived, but you never heard such moaning and groaning at the enforced confinement. As you can probably tell from the noise, they're all happy to be out and about."

"I can tell." She smiled. "If you have no plans for dinner, we'd love to have you join us."

"That would be great. I'll need to drive one of the wagons back, and then I'll be there."

"If you want to ride one of the horses over, I thought we could go for a ride after dinner."

Surprise flicked over him. He'd been trying to get Livvy to go riding for several years and she always made some excuse not to go. Maybe he'd imagined her shyness around horses.

"That sounds great to me."

"Good. See you later." A flash of a smile, and she sailed around the building and through the side door.

Charles grinned and filed into the church behind Jeremiah and Roger. Jeremiah had been unusually quiet since the episode in the barn. He could only hope the boy was reflecting on his actions.

To Charles's relief, the children were on their best behavior. During the song service, he was hard put to concentrate on the songs. As lovely as they were, his glance kept going to Olivia at the piano. Now why couldn't he keep his eyes off her? It was true that she was pretty, with her reddish-gold curls peeking out from beneath the tiny hat atop her head. And when she glanced up, the blue of her eyes sparkled like sapphires. But he and Livvy had never been more than friends. She was like a younger sister to him.

Feeling a little dazed, he gave his head a quick shake and glanced down at the hymnbook. He peered at the page, opened his mouth and his loud baritone swelled out with the words "Shall we gather at the river, where bright angels' feet have trod." A giggle from the girls seated in front of him and the incredulous frown from the song leader was his first indication that something was wrong.

Little by little it seeped into his head and ears that the congregation was singing "Rescue the Perishing."

With an embarrassed attempt at an apologetic smile, Charles found the correct page and cleared his throat before joining in. His burning ears were a sure sign that his face was red as a ripe tomato.

During the rest of the service he sat stiffly and stared at Reverend Shepherd instead of the good reverend's daughter.

After the final prayer, he stood. Maybe he could get out of the building without talking to anyone. A loud burst of laughter near the door caused him to cringe.

Trent and Abigail walked past as he was about to slip

from the pew. Trent, carrying their baby, chuckled, but Abigail flashed Charles a grin.

"I always did say you had a strong voice, Charles," she whispered. Pressing her lips together, she walked away with her husband.

Livvy appeared at his side. "Don't pay any attention to them. I'm going to slip out the side door and help Mama get things ready for dinner. And I happen to know she's made a pecan pie especially for you."

Charles watched her walk away, then, feeling better, he sauntered out the door, pausing to shake hands with Reverend Shepherd. No one gave him a second look. Good. He'd let his imagination run away with him. He headed for the wagon, calling for Sonny and Tommy, who were the only ones who weren't waiting by the wagons where they were supposed to be. By the time the other students were seated, the two rushed up and crawled inside the second wagon.

"Where did you boys take off to?"

"Huntin' cougars," Tommy said. "I know they're out there somewhere."

After a lighthearted, laughter-filled ride home, Charles saddled up Toby, the chestnut gelding, and rode to the parsonage. The thought of going for a ride with Livvy prompted a funny feeling in the pit of his stomach. He gave a short laugh. He had no idea what had gotten into him, but he'd better banish these new and unwelcome ideas if he wanted to maintain his friendship with Livvy. If she knew about the thoughts running through his head, there was no telling what she'd do. But it wouldn't be fun.

He urged Toby into a gallop and rode into the church-yard.

"Livvy, there's another piece of pie in the kitchen. Why don't you get it for Mr. Waverly?"

Livvy stood, but Charles waved her down. "No. No, thank you, Mrs. Shepherd, but I've had two already and, as delicious as it is, I can't eat another forkful of anything."

"Well, then, I'll wrap it up for you to take with you." She stood and headed to the kitchen, apparently intending to make good on her words right away.

Livvy grinned and shook her head at Charles before he could protest. When Mama made up her mind about something, you might as well go along with her.

She was back in a flash. "Now don't let me forget to give it to you when you leave. I know you and Livvy are going riding this afternoon, so I also put a few pieces of chicken in the parcel in case you miss supper at the school."

"That's very kind, Mrs. Shepherd. No one fries chicken like you."

Livvy would just bet he wouldn't say that when Selma was around. She held the title of queen of fried chicken in the entire county.

"I need to change into my riding clothes. I'll be right back."

Quickly she changed into the new wine-colored riding habit and smoothed the hem of the jacket. She pulled on her riding boots and gave herself a once-over in the mirror.

She glanced at the small faux top hat on her dresser. A tiny feather shimmered in the band. Should she? She had a perfectly serviceable riding hat she'd never worn. Was she being vain? With a sudden move, she grabbed it and placed it on top of her head.

Charles urged Toby into a gallop, expecting Livvy to catch up on her little bay mare.

When she didn't pull up beside him, he reined in Toby and waited for her. She threw her head back and laughed, a dimple flashing beside her cute little mouth. Funny, he'd never noticed the dimple before.

"Waiting for me?"

He grinned. "As competitive as you are in other things, I didn't think you'd let me stay ahead of you. By the way, you sit a horse very well. Almost like a professional."

For a moment her face sobered, then she smiled. "My grandfather paid for riding lessons when I was a little girl. I was six when I had my first lesson."

"That was nice of him."

Her lips tightened. "I suppose so."

Curious, he searched her face. "Would you like to stop and talk for a while?"

She hesitated then nodded. "Sure. Let's stop in the peach grove."

He helped her dismount and they secured the horses, then strolled through the grove.

Suddenly, she stopped and looked up at him. "Charles, I need to tell you something."

At the serious look on her face, concern rippled through him. "Is something wrong?"

She sighed and started walking again, her hand brushing against his. Without thinking, her took her hand in his and gave it a gentle squeeze.

"No, nothing is really wrong. Except I'm terrified of horses."

So he'd been right. But this sounded worse than he'd thought. "I'm listening if you'd like to talk about it."

"I believe it's time I did."

"But, Livvy, honey, you were riding just now as though you loved it. I don't understand."

She nodded. "This is the first time in years I've enjoyed riding. I don't understand, either. But trust me, I'm telling you the truth."

"Did something happen to cause this fear?"

She bit her lip. "I loved it the first year of my lessons. Then one day I decided to take the horse out alone. I knew it wasn't allowed, but I did it anyway. We got lost in the woods. Something spooked the horse, and he threw me."

"Were you injured?" The thought of what might have happened made him cringe.

"Just a twisted ankle. But I lay there alone for hours before my father found me. I was terrified. Darkness had begun to fall and I imagined all sorts of wild animals ready to attack."

"That's terrible. What an awful experience for a young child."

She gave another nod. "My grandfather insisted that I get back on the horse the following day, and Father agreed. Although he realized later that it might not have been the right thing to do. They meant well."

He frowned. "Then why in the world did you volunteer to teach riding lessons to the girls?"

"They wanted it so badly and I felt you were being unfair to them. Once I'd volunteered, I was determined to see it through." She threw him a quick glance. "Still am."

He shook his head. "I don't know, Livvy. This might not be a good idea."

"Charles, I told you because, since you're in charge of the riding lessons, I felt you had a right to know. I'm a good rider and perfectly capable of teaching the class. I plan to keep the lessons simple." She shot him a glare. "And you've already agreed to it."

He threw his hands up. "All right, all right. Don't get riled. I'm not going to change my mind. But promise me that if you have any problems you'll come to me."

Tenderness slid across her face. She reached her hand up and touched his cheek. "I promise."

He took her hand and pressed his lips to her palm, then quickly released it. Now why in the world had he done that?

Livvy trembled as she removed the saddle from the huge horse. Well, at the moment the small bay mare seemed huge. Livvy was glad that Hank was at his sister's house today. She needed these few moments alone.

At least, thanks to Trent and Abigail's recent help, she'd made it through the ride without humiliating herself.

Relief coursed through her now that she was no longer keeping her secret from Charles. Although she knew her fear wouldn't cause any problems or danger for the girls, she still felt he had the right to know.

He'd been so concerned and gentle with her, but he'd stood back and let her mount her horse without assistance when they left the grove. He wouldn't coddle her and she was glad about that.

She finished caring for the mare, and headed for the house. Mama was a little nervous about her riding again, but she could tell that Father was relieved. He'd encouraged her to ride for years, but he'd never pushed her.

Thank You Lord, for giving me courage today.

She pushed open the back screen door and went inside.

Chapter 9

The ruler hit the desk with a loud whack, the sound reverberating through the room. Lily Ann jumped up from her desk with a gasp, then sank slowly back to her seat. But few of the children had enough hearing to be affected at all, which made the act useless.

Charles sighed. He didn't often lose his temper and shouldn't have this time. But the children were restless and uncooperative. Had been all morning.

He stepped over to Lily Ann's desk and placed his hand on her shoulder, smiling contritely. "I'm sorry, Lily Ann. You didn't do anything wrong. I just lost my head a little bit."

She grinned. "Those boys are being terrible today, aren't they?"

"Yes, and a couple of the girls are going right along with them."

She nodded, her braids bobbing and face solemn. "You should make them all stay in after school this afternoon."

He chuckled. "You're probably right. But I think I'd rather just send them outside and let them run off some of their energy."

He walked over to one of the front desks and asked Molly to gather up the assignments. As soon as she'd handed them to him and he had them stacked, the class settled down in anticipation of being dismissed for lunch.

Charles raised a hand to get their attention. At the serious look on his face, a few of the students had the grace to appear embarrassed. "Boys and girls," he began. Enunciating carefully and signing as well, he reprimanded them for their behavior and said that most of them deserved detention.

Faces crumpled and a few groans rent the air.

Charles let them think about it for a few minutes. "However, consider this your only warning. Next time will result in staying after school at the end of the day and extra chores."

Relief washed over their faces and they perked up.

"Now everyone line up at the door quietly and in order. It's almost time to go."

They scrambled to obey, and Charles went to the front of the line to get their attention once more. "Remember, no running in the halls." He gave a nod to the girl who was door monitor today. She opened it, then stood with her back against it as the rest of the students filed past her.

As the last of the children scurried downstairs to wash their hands before the meal, Charles sat at his desk for a moment of silence.

Now that the hectic morning was over, a spear of excitement shot through him. Livvy would be here after the noon meal to teach the girls' first riding lesson. Maybe she'd let him observe. Nah, better not ask. But maybe he could sneak a look or two.

A rumble in his stomach reminded him that the students would be lining up by the dining room door. He stood and sauntered down to the main foyer where boys and girls were already standing on the shining hardwood floor in two orderly lines.

The delicious aroma of Selma's chicken and dumplings tantalized his taste buds. He was also hoping for pecan or apple pie today.

Howard, the boys' dorm parent, stood at the head of the boys' line, so Charles took the rear.

Sonny turned his head and gave him a grin. "Sorry we were bad in class, Mr. Charles."

"You weren't bad, Sonny. But you did misbehave. I'm sure you won't do it again."

"No, sir! Don't want them extra chores."

"Those extra chores."

"Yep, sure don't want 'em."

Charles grinned and started to ruffle the boy's hair, but thought better of it. It lay neat for a change. He grinned and gave a gentle pull to Sonny's ear instead.

Within a few minutes, everyone was seated and two servers with white aprons and their heads tied up with white scarves, entered, each carrying a container of soup. Gumbo, Charles hoped. Sissy lifted the lid on hers and started down the table. The smell of creole spices, tomato and okra floated through the room. Charles grinned in appreciation. There was nothing that satisfied his palate quite like Georgia gumbo.

Sissy grinned as she ladled the stew into his bowl. "Here you go, Mr. Charles, especially for you. Cook say so herself."

"Well, tell Cook I give her my humble thanks. I've been yearning for it for three weeks now."

Her cocoa-colored face shone, and she giggled. "It only

been two weeks since she made it last, Mr. Charles. You know that."

"Well, it seems much longer."

Charles loved the lighthearted banter around the table. The children and staff ate together for the midday meal and it seemed that everyone went out of their way to make it a happy time. Or maybe it was a happy time because of the children. They did tend to lighten the mood.

Molly Flannigan's hand shot up.

"Yes, Molly?" Hannah Wilson responded.

"I have a question for Mr. Charles."

Charles looked over and smiled. "And that would be me. How may I help you, Miss Molly?"

She giggled. "Do we get to ride the horses today?"

"I'm sorry. I don't know the answer to that. I'm not sure what Miss Olivia has planned for your first lesson. But I rather doubt it."

"Oh." She drooped a little, and then bounced back up with her usual smile. "But we'll probably get to pet the horses."

Another hand shot up. Margaret Long stared straight at him, her hand waving.

"Yes, Margaret."

"I already know how to ride quite well."

"Yes, I know that. Perhaps you can be helpful to Miss Olivia."

"Yes, sir, I'd be happy to." The thirteen-year-old settled down in her seat with a smug, but happy, look and leaned over to sign to Trudy and Molly.

Charles sighed. The girl was much improved from last year. But she still thought an awful lot of herself. He hoped she wouldn't be any trouble to Olivia.

Just as the meal was ending, Livvy arrived, sweeping into the foyer with a flash of deep red and a burst of autumn air. Before Charles could go to her, she was surrounded by her six new students. A twinge of disappointment bit at him. Ah, well. Perhaps it would be best if he spoke to her after the lesson. But he'd keep an eye on her while she was near the horses.

"Girls, girls, let me catch my breath for a minute." Livvy's laugh tinkled through the hall.

She glanced around in search of Charles and watched him disappear up the staircase. Her heart fell. She'd thought, or at least hoped, that he'd want to be there for her first class, but apparently not. She sucked in her breath. She should be happy that he trusted her to do the job without him. Still…

She led the girls outside to the stables, where Albert had two sidesaddles set up on sawhorses. The smell of hay and old leather, tinged with the sharp smell of manure, wafted across the expanse of the room.

"Are those our saddles?" Trudy's brow wrinkled.

"Yes, aren't they nice?"

Doubt clouded the girl's face. "I guess so. But why can't we ride the regular ones?"

"Because we're young ladies, silly." Margaret tossed her head and gave her friend a look of disdain.

Sensing an impending cat fight, Livvy quickly walked over to the saddles and ran her hand down the side of one. Stopping at the stirrup, she turned and smiled. "If you will all pay close attention, I'd like to teach you a little history about the sidesaddle. Would you believe the first usable one didn't have a stirrup?"

"Where'd they put their feet?" At Lily Ann's query, Livvy remembered the child's plight.

"Come here, Lily. You can use your hands to see the parts of the saddle and bridle while I teach."

Lily quickly complied and reached her hand out. Livvy guided her hand to feel the saddle, then the stirrup.

"Way back in the fourteenth century, a lady called Anne of Bohemia invented the first usable sidesaddle. It was really more like a chair that sat on the horse than a saddle. The rider sat sideways. A footstool was attached for the rider's feet."

Laughter exploded from the girls. Livvy sucked in a breath of relief. Good. Laughter was much better than arguing.

"Remember that name, girls. We might have a test later on."

At the communal groan, she laughed. "I'm just teasing. But there will be a test on the parts of the saddle and bridle and how to place them on the horse."

"When did they invent this kind, with stirrups and all?"

"Not that long ago, Molly. In fact it was earlier this century, but before that, there were better ones than the one Anne invented." She tapped her finger against her chin. "Let's see. In the sixteenth century Catherine de Medici invented one where the rider sat forward with her leg wrapped around the pommel."

"Just one pommel?" Lily Ann touched both pommels on the sidesaddle.

"Yes, I think there was a horn there to rest her knee against. The two-pommel design that we use now was invented in 1830 by Jules Pellier. One pommel is nearly vertical. But look at the second one. It curves downward. Would anyone care to guess why?"

"It curves over the left thigh."

"That is correct, Margaret. The right thigh goes between the two pommels and wraps around, but the left leg hangs downward with the foot on the single stirrup. That curved pommel barely touches the left thigh. That left pommel gave women more security and freedom of movement."

"When my mother was young and lived in England, she used to go fox hunting." Margaret's eyes were wide with excitement. "She said the extra pommel kept her from falling off the horse."

"Very interesting, Margaret. Perhaps your mother would like to visit us one day and tell us about it."

She shrugged. "She's traveling in France with my father."

"I see. Well, maybe when she returns."

Livvy spent the next fifteen minutes or so teaching about the harness, then it was time to saddle and bridle one of the horses.

As Albert led a small chestnut mare named Suzie from her stall, Livvy took a deep breath. *You can do this. God, help me.* She'd practiced at home every day, and had few problems. No nausea, no uncontrolled trembling.

She reached out and ran her hand down the mare's side, murmuring and petting. Then one by one, she allowed the girls to touch and pet the horse.

After the girls each had their turn, she asked them to step back and she showed them how to place and secure the sidesaddle.

As she tightened the girth underneath the horse behind the front legs, she heard a gasp.

"Miss Livvy, won't that hurt her?" Molly's eyes were wide and full of distress. "Will she be able to breathe?"

"I promise she'll breathe just fine, sweetie. While the girth restricts a horse's movements a little, it doesn't hurt at all."

"Really, Molly, don't be silly." Margaret snorted.

"Please don't be unkind, Margaret. Molly was simply concerned. There's nothing silly about that."

A blush tinted the girl's cheeks. "Sorry, Molly."

Molly smiled. "It's okay. I'm not mad."

Livvy shook her head. Molly and Trudy stood up to Margaret more than they used to, but Molly was such a sweet child, she still tended to let the other girl get away with a lot. Livvy sighed. She supposed that was love and forgiveness in action.

She got through the lesson without too many problems. Her hand may have trembled slightly a time or two, but she felt no real fear around the dainty little mare. Lucky for her the sidesaddles were made for smaller horses so at least she didn't have to contend with the large ones.

Once Suzie was back in her stall with an apple as a prize for being so good, Livvy and the girls returned to the house.

"You promise to be back Friday?" Lily Ann asked.

"I promise."

"And we get to ride next time?"

"Yes, Trudy, I think you'll have a few minutes each on a horse on Friday."

As the girls ran upstairs, Livvy glanced around once more for Charles but saw no sign of him. But school hadn't been dismissed yet and she had no real reason to stay. She had hoped to speak with him, though.

Hannah, the sign-language teacher and Lily Ann's mentor, appeared in the foyer.

"Livvy, how did Lily Ann do with the horses?"

"Well, actually, she helped me to put the girth on Suzie, so she could feel how it goes. She seemed fine. Why?" Her face suddenly felt drained and she gasped. "Oh, Hannah, I didn't even think."

Lily Ann's blindness had occurred several years ago, when a runaway horse kicked her in the head. It would have been perfectly normal for the child to have been afraid to go near horses. Livvy felt like kicking herself for being so concerned about her own foolish fears.

Hannah smiled and patted Livvy on the shoulder. "Lily Ann is very strong. I'm happy to hear there were no problems. I'll see you at church Sunday." Hannah headed up the stairs.

With a sigh, Livvy got in her buggy and drove home.

Chapter 10

"Calvin, have you seen Jeremiah?" Charles had looked all over the building to no avail and concern tightened his stomach.

The boy's hands flew. Quite an accomplishment for only a year of signing classes. "Yes, sir. He said he was going out to muck the stable, so Albert wouldn't have to do it."

Warmth rose up in Charles's chest. Jeremiah was a changed boy. He'd been performing little acts of kindness on his own recently. Charles couldn't help the pride that surged through him.

He grinned and gave Calvin a friendly clap on the shoulder, then turned and headed across the still-green lawn to the stable. Jeremiah deserved a reward. Maybe ice cream at the hotel in Magnolia Junction.

He stepped into the stable to find Albert, shovel in hand, scooping manure out of a stall. Confused, he glanced around. "Where's Jeremiah? I thought he was doing that."

"Saw him going in the barn a while back. He sure not doin' this."

Calvin must have misunderstood him. He was probably cleaning the barn instead. Charles tossed a wave at Albert and walked toward the weathered structure that now housed only the cows.

The acrid smell of smoke greeted him as he drew near the building. Dread clutched him. He ran. A vision of Jeremiah, passed out from smoke inhalation while the barn burned, attacked his senses. *God, please let him be all right.*

Charles burst through the barn door. A faint scurrying sound in the rear drew his attention. "Jeremiah?"

He rounded the last stall. Disappointment hit him so hard that nausea washed over him. Jeremiah was stubbing out a cigar and trying unsuccessfully to hide the evidence as he looked up at Charles.

"It's no use. I've already seen it."

Jeremiah swallowed hard, guilt all over his countenance. But not for long. His face stiffened with rebellion and he shrugged, hopping up from the ground and brushing off his overalls.

Charles's jaw tightened and heat rose in his face. He clamped his teeth together. There was no way he could talk to Jeremiah yet.

Finally, he swallowed and took a deep breath. "Meet me in the science room in one hour."

The boy's eyes flashed. "Yes, sir!"

Charles spun on his heel and stalked into the house. He had to get his anger under control. He'd never been one to lose his temper, but the sight of Jeremiah with the cigar had made him see red.

"Mr. Charles, you okay?"

He waved and nodded at Virgie as he passed her in the foyer, then climbed the stairs to the third floor.

The science room was hot and oppressive. You'd think the second week in October would be a little cooler. He sighed. Sinking into his chair behind the desk, he leaned back and closed his eyes. Jeremiah had been doing so well. Charles had worked carefully with the boy, guiding him along. And he'd shown so much promise. Now this.

Is that why you're angry? Because you took pride in Jeremiah's new outlook and attitudes?

The thought hit him hard. Was that it? Did he feel Jeremiah had let him, Charles, down? But then, that didn't say much for his concern for the boy, did it?

Father, forgive me. And please give me wisdom in handling this new situation.

Peace washed over him as the anger drained away. Okay. Obviously Jeremiah needed discipline for smoking. It was not only against the rules, but also a fire hazard. But Charles needed to handle the situation with firmness and love.

By the time Jeremiah tapped on the door, Charles was ready. He hoped. He'd simply have to trust God to lead him.

The boy slipped in, walked board-straight to the front of the desk and stood looking straight into Charles's eyes. It was almost as if he dared him to do something. What in the world did he expect him to do? Throw him in a dungeon or something?

"I'm sure it's not necessary for me to say how disappointed I am, Jeremiah." He paused, but when the boy didn't respond, he went on. "Smoking is against the rules for several reasons. First of all, it's not a healthy choice for a lad your age. Second, it is a fire hazard. But even if these things weren't true, you've broken a school rule."

"So beat me and get it over with."

Charles looked at him in surprise. "Beat you? I would think by now you would know we don't discipline that way."

Something moved in the boy's eyes. Relief? Disbelief?

"We do, however, take rule-breaking seriously. I've decided you will be confined to your room except for school, church and meals for one week. At church, you will remain next to me, as you will at mealtime."

Something like panic clouded the boy's eyes. "Horseback riding? That's school, right?"

Sympathy slid over Charles. He knew how much the horses meant to Jeremiah. "Sorry. No horses until the week is over."

"That's not fair! It's a school lesson."

"Jeremiah, it's not a regular school course. It's a privilege. You know that. So don't argue, please."

Thunder raged in the boy's eyes. "May I go now?"

"Yes, you're dismissed. Please go straight to your room."

Jeremiah spun around and stalked out of the science room. His footsteps resounded as he stomped down the hall to the stairs.

Charles took a deep breath and stepped over to the window. Some of the trees were beginning to turn color. The sight of them usually gave him peace. There was something about a touch of autumn that sent joy surging through him. But not today. His heart raged with pain. Oh, Jeremiah would eventually get over this. But the anger in Jeremiah's eyes surely wasn't just from being deprived of horseback riding for a week.

He left the room and walked down the stairs. When he reached the second floor, he turned left to go check out Jeremiah and make sure he was in his room. Standing outside the door, he could hear something hitting the wall inside the room. Charles stood still. It sounded as if someone was throwing things all over the place. When there was no pause in the sounds inside, he turned the doorknob and entered.

Books lay scattered all over the floor. Jeremiah, shirt ripped off, was in the process of throwing a glass-framed picture against the wall. Apparently, he'd already broken at least one because shattered glass crackled beneath Charles's boots.

When Jeremiah saw Charles, he glared and turned to grab another book.

Charles gasped. Welts and scars crisscrossed Jeremiah's back and shoulders.

Jeremiah whirled and grabbed a shirt. Shame filled his eyes as he put it on and buttoned it up.

"Spy! Why are you spying on me?" he lashed out with a pain-filled voice.

"I'm sorry, Jeremiah. I didn't mean to spy." Horror filled his heart. *God, how do I handle this without hurting him more?* "Come on. Let's get this room cleaned up. I don't think you want to spend a week in the middle of this mess."

"You don't have to help." His voice was choked. "I did it. I'll fix it."

"But I don't mind helping. And when we're done, perhaps you can tell me how you got those scars on your back and who did it to you?"

Jeremiah glared and blinked back the tears that threatened to overflow his warm brown eyes. "None of your business."

Charles walked over and touched him on the arm. "Yes, it is. Someone has been horribly cruel to you and that certainly is my business."

Jeremiah blinked and began cleaning the shattered room. In silence they worked side by side until the room showed a semblance of neatness. A pile of refuse in the corner was the only evidence of the rage that had been vented there.

Finally, shoulders sagging, Jeremiah glanced at Charles. "I can't talk about it. He said he'd hurt someone if I did."

Charles dragged a chair over with his foot and shoved it toward Jeremiah, then got another one from the corner. When they were both seated, Charles waited.

"Did you hear me? He said he'd hurt someone."

Charles shoved down the anger that threatened to well up within him at the thought of what someone had put a child through. And from the looks of his scars, it had been going on for some time.

He took a deep breath. "I can understand your fright over the situation, Jeremiah. You're worried about someone you care about. Evil people who torture children usually use this tactic to keep their victims quiet. And fifty years ago, you'd have had reason to be afraid. But times have changed. There are laws now to protect citizens, especially children, from violence."

A glimmer of hope shone in Jeremiah's eyes. "Are you sure?"

"I'm very sure. But I need to know who is guilty and who is being threatened."

"It was my uncle. And he threatened my ma."

"It must have been hard for you to hear this, Charles."

Charles stood from the chair in front of P.H.'s desk and paced the room. "It was. But that doesn't matter. The important thing is to put that man in jail and put a stop to it."

"Are you sure that's possible? At this point, it might be Jeremiah's word against his uncle's."

Charles froze. What if she was right?

Sympathy crossed the director's face. "Don't worry. If

legal channels don't take care of the matter, we'll think of something else." She tapped her fingers on the oak desk. "If nothing else, we can help Jeremiah's mother get away from the man."

"I need to take a trip right away and check on the mother."

P.H. nodded. "Not alone. I'll see if Trent can get away."

"Since he was nine years old, P.H. He's been going through it that long." A shudder ran through Charles's body. "How can anyone be such a monster?"

"I don't know. But you need to get yourself together before you see Jeremiah again. Why don't you take a ride over to Olivia's?"

Charles gave P.H. a quick glance. The thought had already crossed his mind, but why would P.H. think Livvy could calm him?

He rose. "I think I will. Should I stop by Trent's?"

"No, I'll talk to him at church tomorrow and find out the soonest he can get away."

"Send someone to check on Jeremiah, will you?"

"I'll go myself and take him some lemonade and cookies."

Relief washed over Charles. P.H. was a tenderhearted and godly woman besides being an excellent director. What had they ever done without her?

Livvy drowsed in the porch swing, allowing the breeze to move the swing. She really needed to go over her Sunday school lesson one more time, but it was so peaceful to linger here.

She jerked her head up at the sound of horse's hooves pounding up the drive. Delighted to see Charles, she stepped to the edge of the porch and waited, smiling, while he reined his horse in, dismounted and tied the reins. It was only when he turned and started for the porch that she saw the expression on his face.

Before she could question him, he was on the porch and holding her closely. Shock jolted through her at his nearness and the fact that he'd never done more than hold her hand before. Something was wrong.

She wrapped her arms around him and ran her hand across his back as his shoulders shook with silent sobs.

Finally, he raised his head. "You must think I'm the biggest crybaby in the world. This isn't the first time I've cried on your shoulder."

Livvy drew back and peered into his eyes. "I know you're not a crybaby, Charles. You have always seemed very masculine to me."

He smiled. "That's a relief to know. I was beginning to wonder myself." He ran his thumb down her cheek then led her over to the swing. "But these tears weren't for me, Livvy."

"What's wrong?"

Livvy listened in horror as Charles related the smoking episode. When he went on to tell her about seeing the scars on Jeremiah's back, she gasped.

"Oh, Charles, how terrible. No wonder the poor boy is so troubled. Did you find out who is responsible?"

"Yes. Jeremiah's father was killed in a farm accident when the boy was only nine. Shortly afterward, his father's brother moved in, bag and baggage, and took over the farm as well as his brother's wife and child. He's basically held a rod over both their heads in exchange for allowing them to stay in their own home."

"And he's beaten them both all this time?" Pain stabbed through her at the thought.

"Jeremiah said he doesn't think his uncle, Ed, ever laid a hand on his mother. But he thrashed Jeremiah unmercifully for every small offense. Sometimes for no offense at all. Jeremiah's mother went behind the man's back to make arrangements for Jeremiah's enrollment at Quincy. But the uncle threatened the boy with harm to his mother if he ever told anyone about the beatings."

Livvy couldn't suppress the moan that escaped her lips. "What do you intend to do about it?"

Satisfaction ran through Charles that Livvy knew he'd do something about the situation. "My first instinct was to hop the next train to Severn's Flat and beat the tar out of the monster. But P.H. convinced me otherwise."

"I should think she would."

"She's going to talk to Trent tomorrow and see how soon he can get away so we can go together. That way we'll have each other as witnesses in case the man tries to pull a fast one."

"So what is the plan?"

"I think the first thing we need to do is speak to Jeremiah's mother, but Trent and I will decide together what further course of action to take. If the sheriff refuses to cooperate, we might need an attorney."

"But that man won't get his hands on Jeremiah?" Livvy trembled at the thought.

"No. I can promise you that."

"What about the farm? Does Jeremiah's uncle have any legal right to that?"

"I'm not sure what the circumstances are. That'll be another case for an attorney. It would be nice if they could have it returned to them. But, again, I don't really know the circumstances. Jeremiah's father might have willed it to his brother. We'll have to see."

He stood and lifted Livvy to stand beside him. "You're always good for me, Livvy. I don't know what I'd do without you."

Warmth slid across her face at the tenderness in his voice and the look in his eyes. If she didn't know better, she'd almost think he loved her. *Stop it, Livvy. You do know better.* And her feelings didn't matter now, anyway. Jeremiah's problem was the only thing that mattered. But as Charles rode away in the dusky twilight, her heart twisted with yearning. If only…

Chapter 11

The busy station teemed with waiting passengers as Charles and Trent stepped down from the train in Rome, Georgia. There was no railway service to Severn's Flat, so they'd need to rent a couple of horses. They'd come prepared, the few belongings they'd need in saddlebags now thrown over their shoulders. Charles readjusted his as they walked down the dusty street.

They found the livery stable around the corner from the depot. Within moments, they had gotten directions to the small community of Severn's Flat.

The scrawny, bearded man running the livery leaned against the door frame and scratched his chin. "Now, purty soon, you'll come acrost this here sign where the road veers off two ways. The way the sign pints leads to the feed store and grocer in Severn's Flat. Don't go that way. Take the other d'rection and ye'll end up at the Saunders' farm."

They headed out of town and soon saw the sign veering in two directions.

Charles grinned and motioned down one branch of the road. "The sign's pintin' that way so I reckon we best go the other."

"I reckon." Trent laughed. "I love the colorful speech of this region. It'll be lost one day."

Tense with anticipation of what might happen at the Saunders' farm, Charles tried to relax by enjoying the fall colors. Seemingly overnight, flaming reds and oranges had sprung forth. They wouldn't last long, though. A couple of weeks, maybe, then the first hard rain would knock them off their branches to carpet the ground.

They rounded a bend in the road and both slowed their mounts as a neat, white house came into view. Clothing blew in the breeze on a line that ran between two posts.

A brown-and-white dog charged down the steps and ran toward them, barking.

As they pulled up in front of the house, the front door opened and a small-framed woman with a heart-shaped face stepped out onto the porch. A large bruise on her cheek marred the smooth skin. Worried brown eyes peered at them, then recognition filled them and she set down the rifle she'd held in both hands.

"Jeremiah?" she cried in a choked voice. "Is something wrong with my boy?"

Charles glanced quickly at Trent, not wanting to overstep his authority.

"No, no." Trent dismounted quickly and went to meet her, taking both her hands in his. "Jeremiah is fine."

"Then why are you here? Do I owe you money or something?"

Charles dismounted and joined them.

"No, Mrs. Saunders. You don't owe us anything. We merely need to talk to you about a matter that concerns us."

"Very well." She motioned toward the door. "Won't you come in, please?"

As soon as they were settled in the parlor with mugs of boiling-hot coffee, Trent cleared his throat. "Is your brother-in-law here?"

A shadow crossed her face. "No, he took some cattle to Atlanta to an auction today. He won't be home until late. Do you have business with him?"

Trent cleared his throat. "Not at all. We need to speak to you uninterrupted, so it's good that he's not here." He nodded toward Charles. "I'm sure you recognize Mr. Waverly, our science teacher."

She nodded. "Yes. How is Jeremiah doing with his classes, Mr. Waverly?"

"Very well. I'm pleased with his progress. And he's wonderful with the horses."

"Yes, he was so happy when he wrote to me about the riding lessons. When he rides, it's almost as if he's part of the horse."

Charles laughed. "My thoughts, exactly."

He glanced at Trent who nodded for him to continue.

"Mrs. Saunders, are you aware that your son has scars all over his back and shoulders?"

Her face paled and she gasped, closing her eyes for a moment. "Yes," she whispered.

"Jeremiah said his uncle has beaten him for years."

"Yes." Tears overflowed her eyes. "It's true. I tried to stop him, but he's such a big man. I was so thankful when Jeremiah had the opportunity to go to school. Not only to learn, but to get away from Edward."

Trent leaned forward. "You do realize that something needs to be done about it?"

"But what? He's taken the farm and threatens to kick us out. I can't allow my son to be homeless."

"If you don't mind my asking, how did he get control of the farm? Did your husband leave it to him?"

Confusion clouded her face. "Frank told me once he'd seen a lawyer and had a will drawn up so if anything happened to him, the farm would go to me, then on to Jeremiah. He showed me a piece of paper and said he'd keep it in the cash box."

"Do you not have the will?"

"No. After my husband died, Edward showed up one day and said he'd help me with the farm. I thought he was being kind, but then he told me that Frank had left all the property to him, but not to worry. He'd take care of us." A sob escaped her lips. "I looked and looked but couldn't find the will Frank had told me about. He might have changed his mind."

Charles glanced at Trent who returned his look, his lips tight. "That might be so, Mrs. Saunders, but then again, your husband's brother could be lying and trying to steal your inheritance."

She nodded. "I think that's very possible, but I have no idea what to do about it."

"Did he ever mention the attorney's name?"

She shook her head. "I've no idea."

Charles couldn't stand it any longer. He had to know. "Has your brother-in-law been hitting you, too? I couldn't help noticing the bruise on your face."

A blush covered her face and she ducked her head and nodded.

Trent drew in a breath. "Why don't you pack up some things and come back to the school with us? There are several vacant bedrooms and you'd be welcome."

She froze and her eyes widened. "Oh, no. If I do that, he'll have the property free and clear and Jeremiah will never receive the inheritance his father left for him." She rose, trembling.

"Mrs. Saunders, I promise I will obtain an attorney to look into this matter. And there's also the matter of the beatings. There are laws against child beating now, and the man needs to be in jail."

"But what if they don't put him there? What if he goes after Jeremiah and hurts him worse?"

Charles stepped to her side. "I promise you that is not going to happen. Whatever happens with the farm, Edward Saunders will never lay a hand on that boy again."

A faint ray of hope jumped into her eyes. "What do you intend to do?"

"First, we need to take you to the school, where you'll be safe. Then I think the next step has to be to consult Trent's attorney. Once he looks into things, he can advise us on a course of action. I would say that unless your brother-in-law has proof that the property was left to him, he hasn't a legal leg to stand on."

"All right, but if I take the carriage, he might say I've stolen it."

Trent sent her a look of sympathy. "Pack what you can in a carpetbag. If you don't mind riding behind one of us to the train, that would be the simplest way."

"I don't mind at all."

She glanced from one to the other, gratitude shining in her eyes. "Don't let him rob my boy. This is all he has left of his father."

Livvy tried to keep her eyes on the piano, but her glance kept straying to the very pretty and petite lady who sat between Charles and Jeremiah.

Really, she was being so foolish to think that Charles might be attracted to Jeremiah's mother. The woman must be in her thirties. The problem was that she didn't look any older than Livvy. She took a deep breath. Would he still come to dinner? Or would he choose to eat at the school today?

The smell of liniment hit her and she crinkled her nose. Old Mrs. Henderson's rheumatism must be acting up again.

She jerked her attention back to the hymnal and finished the song. The song leader stepped down from the platform and her father took his place behind the pulpit. At a nod from him, she rose and seated herself on the front row beside her mother.

A big smile creased her father's face. "Today, it's my honor to welcome Jeremiah Saunders's mother to our service. It's nice to have you with us, Mrs. Saunders."

She gave a slight nod and murmured something so quietly Livvy couldn't make it out. Goodness. Couldn't the woman even speak up?

Shame coursed through her. She wouldn't do this again. She wouldn't make an enemy in her own mind as she'd done with Helen. If Charles was interested in Mrs. Saunders, she'd simply have to live with it.

When the service ended, Livvy made a beeline for Jeremiah's mother. The faint aroma of apple blossoms surrounded the lady. Livvy held her hand out. "How do you do, Mrs. Saunders? I'm Olivia Shepherd, the reverend's daughter. It's so nice you can be here with Jeremiah today." She glanced toward the beaming boy. "And it's obvious he's overjoyed."

"Oh, yes. But no more than I am." The lady smiled at her son, then turned back to Livvy. "And please call me Faith."

"I will, if you will call me Livvy." She smiled warmly at Faith, surprised to find the warmth extending to her heart. *Thank You, Lord.*

Charles stepped to Livvy's side and gave her a grin. "Am I still invited to dinner?"

Her stomach lurched. He hadn't forgotten. "Of course. Mama made a pork roast with sweet potatoes and one of your favorite pies."

"Pecan?"

"Pecan." She laughed, then turned to Faith. "You're welcome to join us, if you'd like. Mama always makes plenty."

"That's kind of you, but I promised Jeremiah to sit with him at dinner and he wants me to try Selma's famous fried chicken."

"You won't be sorry. She's a whiz in the kitchen." Livvy held her hand out and Faith took it in her small one. "Perhaps another time."

Livvy hurried home to help her mother finish up the dinner preparations. Her heart thudded when she heard hooves pounding up the drive. Quickly, she removed her apron and smoothed down her hair.

After dinner and dishes, Charles and Livvy walked down by the river and sat under their favorite live oak.

"Did you find out anything about the abuse?" Livvy's voice trembled just saying the words.

Charles nodded. "It was the uncle all right. He started beating the kid as soon as he took over the farm. Not only that, but he claims the farm is his."

Livvy looked up, startled. "Is it?"

"I doubt it. According to Mrs. Saunders, her husband told her he'd made out a will leaving everything to her and Jeremiah. But the will seems to have disappeared and she doesn't know the name of the attorney who took care of the matter."

"Oh, no. Can anything be done?"

"Trent has his lawyer looking into it. If anyone can find out anything, Jack Taylor will."

"Charles, has that man been hitting Faith, too? She has a bruise on her cheek."

"Apparently, yes." He reached over and ran a thumb down her cheek. "Don't worry, we'll get to the bottom of all this."

A thrill ran down Livvy's cheek where he'd touched her. This was the second time he'd done that. Were his feelings for her changing? She snapped back to reality. It wouldn't do to get her hopes up. And it wouldn't do for her to show him how she felt about him.

Charles reached over to stroke Livvy's cheek again, then pulled back. What was he doing? It was a wonder she hadn't slapped him silly. She probably hadn't thought anything of it. Livvy was his best friend and he didn't want to undermine their friendship. But he knew his feelings for her were changing. He'd be an idiot not to realize it.

Hooves pounded up the road and voices shouted.

Charles and Livvy both jumped up and headed for the churchyard.

Ezra Bines and the Hedley boys stood talking to Livvy's father, their hands motioning wildly.

Charles dashed over just as the reverend ran inside the church. "What's going on?" he asked Ezra.

"Woods back of Matt Jenkins's place are on fire. Will you get Trent and Albert and meet us there? We're rounding folks up to help. Bring plows." Ezra and the Hedleys whirled their horses around and galloped down the lane.

The church bell began to ring in loud peals. That would bring people.

"Livvy, I have to go. Ask your father to load up his plow and bring it. I'll swing by the school for Howard and Albert, then ride over to let Trent and Solomon know."

"Be careful, Charles."

He barely heard her whisper, but her face had gone ashen-white. Without thinking, he leaned over and kissed her brow.

He rushed to the stable where Jake had his horse ready. Jumping in the saddle, he bounded down the road.

Livvy stood and stared after him, then realized that Father was driving the wagon out of the barn. He'd tossed both their plows inside. Jake jumped up beside him.

"Father, do you have to go?" Her cry was shrill to her own ears.

"Livvy, they'll need every man and every plow. We have to plow up the pastures to keep them from catching fire." He smiled. "Don't worry. I'll be fine. I've done this dozens of times through the years. Look after your mama until I get back."

"Watch out for him, Jake. Please?"

The kind employee and friend gave her a nod and then they were gone.

Livvy stumbled into the house. Regardless of what Father had said, forest fires were dangerous. Every year she heard of someone getting killed while trying to put out the roaring flames.

The house was silent. Livvy slipped into the parlor where she found her mother on her knees in front of her high-back rocking chair. Her Bible lay open on the seat cushion.

She looked up when Livvy entered. Peace filled her eyes as she rose from the floor.

"Let's go have a cup of tea." She patted Livvy on the shoulder. "How does that sound?"

"All right, Mama."

When they were seated at the kitchen table, Livvy gave her mother a curious glance. "How do you do it, Mama?"

"Do what, dear?" She set her cup on the table and gave Livvy her attention.

"How do you keep your faith and your peace at times like this?" She bit her lip. "I know you must worry, but somehow, once you pray, the peace is all over you."

Mama reached over and patted Livvy's hand. "It's not always easy, dear. But then I remember—your father is safe in God's hands. No matter what happens, he's safe in God's hands. And that gives me peace."

Chapter 12

"Pa!" Livvy let the screen door slam behind her and ran to the wagon. "Pa, are you all right?"

The smell of smoke and burned wood clung to Father and Jake as they drove the wagon to the barn after midnight.

Pa ran a hand over his eyes then glanced down at her from the wagon seat. "I'm fine, daughter." A smile crossed his face. "You haven't called me *Pa* in ten years. I like it."

Relief washed over Livvy. If Pa was joking, he was all right. "I like it, too. I've no idea why I started saying *Father*. That sounds too formal." Her voice shook. What if something had happened to her father?

She glanced at Jake. "How about you, Jake?"

"I'm just fine, Miss Livvy. Don't go worrying about me." He groaned and stretched his arm above his shoulders. "Mighty tired, though. Think I'll unhitch the mules and go to bed."

"Wouldn't you like a bite to eat?"

"No, thanks."

Pa climbed down from the wagon. "Let's go inside, Livvy. I could use a cup of coffee, if there's any in the pot."

"Yes, sir. Mama insisted on keeping it hot. She's getting food on the table for you now. Chicken soup and hot bread."

"That sounds wonderful."

Livvy swallowed. "Pa, is everyone else all right?"

"Yes, we got the fire under control before it could reach the Jenkins's house, but it was close." Pa cut her a sideways look. "Everyone else is fine as can be. Just tired. He said to tell you, he'll be over after classes tomorrow."

Warmth rushed to Livvy's cheeks. But she flashed a grin at her father. "Can't fool you, can I?"

A laugh rumbled from his throat. "I don't know when you two young people are going to realize you're in love and get on with the business of romance."

"Now, Pa. I'm just a friend to Charles." She sighed. "That's all I've ever been."

"You think so? Well, if you could see the way he looks at you and hear the way he speaks of you when you're not around, you might think otherwise."

Livvy tried to resist the hope that rose in her at Pa's words, but her stomach jumped with excitement.

"Stop dawdling, Livvy." Ma stood in the doorway, her eyes glued to Pa. "Your father needs to get something hot into his stomach and get some rest. It's well after midnight and he's had a hard night."

Pa stepped inside and placed a gentle kiss on Ma's cheek. "You're right, dear. I'm just going to get cleaned up a little first."

Livvy lay in bed for a long time, her father's words about Charles playing in her mind. Was Pa right? Livvy had noticed a change in Charles's attitude toward her lately, but thought she was only imagining things.

Finally, she sank into a peaceful sleep, waking to sunlight streaming through her window and the faint smell of smoke and charred wood in the air.

Ma had two baskets of food ready to take to the Jenkinses'. "I don't imagine Maude will have much time for cooking today with cleaning up the smoke and ash."

"Oh, Ma. I hadn't thought of that. Maybe I should go over and help."

"That would be the neighborly thing to do and I'm sure she'd appreciate it." Ma wiped a strand of hair from her brow. "I'd go myself but I promised to spend the day with Mrs. Waters, so her daughter can go to town for household supplies."

Livvy changed into one of her oldest dresses, then carried the baskets to the buggy with a few things she thought would amuse the children and headed off to the Jenkinses'.

Four small children, covered with soot, played in the front yard. Dotty Jenkins, only six years old, tried, to no avail, to corral them back to the cleared space in front of the house.

"You kids better mind me, now. You know what Ma said."

Livvy suspected the Dotty had been ignoring them until she saw the buggy pull into the yard. "Hi, Dotty. Have your hands full, I see."

The girl sighed. "Oh, these kids. They never mind. Now look at them. Ma and I'll have to do the wash early." With hungry eyes, she gazed at the baskets as Livvy lifted them from the buggy.

Livvy smiled at the younger children who'd gathered around. "I brought picture books. If you'll go scrub those hands good, perhaps we could find a place for you to look at them."

"Aww. Who cares about books?" the only boy in the group retorted.

"Well, one of them has pictures of cows and horses. And one even has a horseless carriage. And if it's all right with your ma to have one, I'm pretty sure there are cookies in one of these baskets."

A gasp showed that he was impressed. He led the pack to the washtub at the back of the house, with Dotty in close pursuit.

The front door opened and Maude stepped onto the porch. Her thin face appeared tired, and discouragement shadowed her eyes.

"Good morning, Maude. I thought you might need some help today." Livvy grinned at her neighbor. "I know I would in your place."

Maude's face lit up. "Oh, Livvy, you are a godsend. I sure can. Miz Wilson and Miz Frank are coming to help out later, but they won't be able to stay long."

"Well, I can stay as long as you need me." Livvy lifted one of the baskets. "Ma sent some stew and cornbread so you wouldn't have to cook dinner. And ham and cold meat loaf and other foodstuffs for later."

"Bless her heart. That is good news. You be sure to thank her for me, now."

"I'm sure the other ladies of the community will bring things, too. Don't you worry." She held up a hand. "Oh, I forgot. Be right back."

She hurried to the buggy and removed four quilts. She offered them to Maude. "Mama thought you might need these until you get a chance to wash and air out your own."

Maude took one of the soft quilts and sank to the top

step. She held the coverlet to her nose and breathed in deeply. Tears spilled and ran down her cheeks.

"Oh, Livvy. Don't think I'm not grateful to God for sparing our place. Because I am. But the constant soot and smoke are about to make me despair."

The sound of hooves and wagon wheels drew their attention and Maude jumped up, wiping her tear-filled eyes and making a sooty smear across her cheek.

Two wagons pulled up. Solomon and Carrie hopped down. Carrie scooped up an armful of rags from behind the seat and Solomon grabbed two large baskets.

"Doc Trent thought maybe Mr. Jenkins could use some help so Solomon came. And Abigail said she could manage without me today, so I came along to help you. She sent a load of food along, too."

Solomon unhitched one of the mules. "Doc said tell you he'd like to be here helping, but got to make rounds today and check on some sick folks." He mounted the mule and took off toward the woods.

Maude grabbed Carrie by the shoulders. "Girl, you are a sight for sore eyes and I do mean sore." She laughed and motioned to her eyes, which were red and watery from smoke and more than likely made worse by crying.

Within an hour, several neighbor ladies had arrived. Even with all the help, the work was tedious, filthy and slow, but they'd begun to see progress by midafternoon. The sound of hooves announced the appearance of another horse and rider.

The sight of Charles sitting tall and strong in the saddle caused Livvy's heart to lurch. He smiled down at her. "I'd have been here earlier, but I had to corral boys all day. I think Jeremiah came early to help Jenkins. I thought I'd better come get him. His mother's getting worried."

Livvy nodded and smiled. "Last time I saw him, he'd finished dinner and was heading back to work with a drumstick in one hand and a fried pie in the other."

Charles threw back his head and laughed. "Is it all right if I come over tonight after supper? Trent heard some news from his lawyer."

"Oh, please do. I can't wait to hear."

Charles waved and rode away and Livvy, with uplifted spirits, went to help clean soot off the Jenkinses's parlor wall.

By the time the day was done, Livvy's muscles screamed with pain. She sighed with relief as she headed home. When she arrived at the parsonage, her mother had a tub of hot water waiting in her bedroom.

"I figured you'd be good and dirty. You run along and take a nice, long soak while I finish up supper."

"How is Mrs. Waters today, Ma?"

"Her rheumatism was acting up a little, but otherwise she had a pretty good day. She even sat at the table to eat her dinner instead of having a tray in bed."

"That's an improvement over last week." Livvy shook her head. "She wanted me to get Pa to read a 'final' scripture over her."

"Well, poor old soul. She's getting up there in years and she knows it." Ma's brow furrowed and she sighed. "You run along now. And take your time."

Livvy went to her room and removed her smoke- and soot-covered clothing, then sank into the still-steaming water. She inhaled the faint aroma of rose water in appreciation and sank lower into the sudsy bath.

Not wanting to leave her mother with all the work, Livvy didn't linger for long. A half hour later, she stepped into the kitchen, clean, refreshed and smiling.

"There. That looks more like my girl." Ma patted her on the shoulder as she sailed past with a platter of hot bread.

"Umm. That cornbread looks so good. Is that chili I smell?"

"Yes, I thought it was a good day for something hot and tasty. Besides, I could simmer it on low all day."

Livvy laughed. "Well, whatever the reason, I'm all for it."

"Why don't you slice the apple pie while I get the chili on the table and we'll be ready."

"Yes, ma'am." Livvy sliced the pie and covered it with a tea towel. She stepped over to the large kitchen table where they ate most of their family meals.

"Charles is coming over after supper. They've had some news from Trent's lawyer."

"That was fast."

"Well, telegrams do make things swifter." Livvy smiled.

"I hope they can do something for that poor lady and her boy. It would be a shame if they lose their farm."

"Well, Trent and Charles will do everything they can to prevent that from happening."

"I'm sure they will. They are honorable gentlemen."

Livvy went to the parlor to get her father. Soon the three of them sat around the table, enjoying the delicious food and delightful family conversation.

When Charles arrived, Mama insisted on giving him a slice of pecan pie from the day before. Although he said he was stuffed from Selma's supper, he managed to scrape the plate clean in no time.

"Selma doesn't make pecan pie very often, Mrs. Shepherd, so this is a rare treat."

She laughed. "That's because the children like fruit pies better and you know how Selma is about those boys and girls."

He laughed. "I know. When they all came back to school after the summer vacation, she made peach pie and peach cobbler nearly every day for the first month. And fried chicken, of course."

After Livvy helped clear away and clean the kitchen, she and Charles stepped out onto the porch.

"Did you want to walk by the river tonight?" Charles asked.

"Heavens, no. I'm all worn-out from working at the Jenkinses'." She motioned toward the porch swing. "Let's sit there and talk."

"Good. I was hoping you'd say that. I'm a little tired tonight myself, although all I did was herd boys all afternoon."

Livvy laughed. "Herd boys? The very idea, Charles."

"Well, that's what it felt like today." He grinned and sat beside her on the swing.

She leaned back and breathed a contented sigh. *Thank You, Lord, for my home, my family and for Charles sitting here beside me with that adorable grin on his handsome face.*

After a moment of drowsy peace, she sat up. "So what did the lawyer say?"

"First of all, he's already found Frank Saunders's attorney and he says he has a copy of the will in his safe. Saunders left the farm to his wife for her lifetime, and then it's to go to Jeremiah."

"Oh, Charles. That is such wonderful news. Mrs. Saunders must be beside herself with happiness."

"She started crying when Trent told her."

"What will they do next?" Livvy could barely contain the joy bubbling inside. She hated it when bullies won.

"Trent is going to ask the attorney and the local sheriff to accompany us to the farm to confront Jeremiah's uncle.

The man has no recourse but to count his losses and leave. I hope he hasn't ruined things for Jeremiah and his mother, such as by putting them in debt."

"That would be terrible. I'll ask Pa and Mama to pray about it, Charles. God has already done so much in the situation, starting with your finding out about Jeremiah's scars. Surely He'll take care of the rest, too."

"Of course He will. He'll take care of it. And thanks for offering to pray."

"You know I was thinking about Jeremiah's bullying of the younger boys and how it was related to his own abuse. I can't help wondering what his uncle might have gone through to make him the way he is."

"Some folks are just mean, Livvy."

"Maybe. Maybe not. I'm certainly not excusing the man. We all have the opportunity to make choices, whether good or bad, and he chose bad ones. Just as Jeremiah did in the beginning. By the way, how is he treating the little ones now?"

"He mostly ignores them. Every now and then he'll pick on them. I haven't noticed him doing it much since his mother arrived. I think having her near is a good influence on him."

"Of course. She's his mother. And I'm sure she's taught him right from wrong."

"I'm sure you're right." He tweaked her nose. "You're so cute when you get excited about something."

Her stomach fluttered and warmth ran from her head to her toes. "Really, Charles. I'm a little old to have my nose tweaked."

"Sorry. Don't know what got into me."

She laughed. "It's all right. I don't mind."

He leaned over and kissed the nose in question. "There, do you mind that?"

Butterflies danced in her stomach, and she leaned back and giggled. "Charles Waverly! What's gotten into you tonight? You aren't coming down with a fever or something, are you?"

"Maybe. Maybe I've been bitten by something." He smiled and stood. "I'd better get home before I make you good and mad."

"I'm not mad. Good night, Charles. Thanks for sharing the news with me. You'll let me know when you hear anything else?"

"Of course." He took her hand and turned it over, then pressed his lips to her palm. Livvy shivered at the unexpected intimacy. When she stood, her knees wobbled and she quickly sat again before he could notice. With another smile, he mounted his horse and rode down the lane.

Chapter 13

Dry leaves crackled beneath the buggy wheels as Livvy drove up the lane to the school. She couldn't prevent the niggle of worry that worked at the edge of her mind.

Where was the rain? There had been two more fires over the past two weeks and she wasn't alone in her concern. She could see it in the fearful glances of her friends and neighbors. It was past time for the rainy season to start, but it had been nearly a month since the one gully washer.

The girls were waiting at the stable, their faces bright with anticipation. Only one had dropped out of the class, stating that she hated riding sidesaddle.

Margaret was the first to get her horse saddled. Livvy nodded with satisfaction as the girl turned to help Lily Ann.

Finally, it was time to mount, and Livvy told Margaret and Brenda to go first. Brenda climbed up on the mounting block but still had trouble reaching the stirrup with her short legs.

A guffaw exploded as Jeremiah pointed at Brenda. "Maybe she needs a ladder."

Livvy's lips tightened and she stalked over to Jeremiah. "Perhaps instead of laughing at the young lady, you could use your mental talents a little better and come up with a solution to Brenda's problem. Lily Ann could use the help, as well."

A stunned look crossed his face. "Yes, ma'am. Sorry." He ducked back into the stable.

She gave a satisfied nod and walked back to the girls.

The ride was uneventful and soon all the girls had had their turn.

When the horses were taken care of and the girls dismissed, Livvy saw Charles standing by her buggy.

"Thanks for getting it ready for me, Charles."

"My pleasure. Thought I'd see you off, since I probably won't see you again until Sunday."

Livvy grinned. "That's only four days away."

"I know. But it seems longer."

Livvy blushed, not sure what to make of his remark. It almost seemed… She cleared her throat. "Jeremiah was teasing the girls this time."

Charles's brow rose in displeasure. "The girls? What was he doing?"

She raised her hand. "Nothing physical. As I said, just teasing."

"He shouldn't be doing that, either. I'll have a talk with him." A frown still creased his brow.

"Oh, please don't, Charles. I think he was ashamed, and he did apologize. I shouldn't have said anything."

"All right. I won't say anything, but let me know if it happens again. I don't want him to fall into his old habits now that his mother isn't here."

"Where is Mrs. Saunders? Did she get everything settled about her farm, then?" How wonderful that would be, if she did.

"No, they're still working on that. Patrick and Helen needed some help at the store so she's working for them and living in the apartment above the shop. She also helps Helen at the house, I believe."

"Oh. That should work well for all of them. She seems independent. I doubt she'd want to have to accept help she hadn't earned for long."

And Helen could more than likely use the help around the house, with her still teaching part-time. Although Abigail had said they had several applicants for Helen's position.

As Livvy drove home, the things on her mind had nothing to do with Helen or Mrs. Saunders. Was Charles beginning to feel something for her besides friendship? Did she dare hope?

Charles watched the back of Livvy's red-gold head as the buggy rounded the curve and disappeared down the lane.

Was there any chance that she might return his feelings or had he waited too long to try to win her? She'd always been there for him, but he'd seen her almost as a younger sister. How could he have been so blind to his own feelings?

He sighed. There was nothing he could do about it yet except for the not-so-subtle hints he'd been dropping. But as soon as this mess with the Saunders family was cleared up and he knew for sure that Jeremiah and his mother were safe from harm, he intended to have a very heart-to-heart talk with Miss Olivia Shepherd.

He sighed and headed for the stable to see if Jeremiah was finished helping Albert. He'd promised Livvy he wouldn't talk to the boy about his teasing, but he could at least keep an eye on him.

He found Albert sitting on a bale of hay drinking apple cider.

Albert motioned to the quart jar beside him. "Have some cider? Got another cup here somewhere."

"No, thanks, Albert. I'm looking for Jeremiah."

"Oh, that boy worked hard today. I tol' him to quit for the day. I think he over at the barn building something." Albert scratched his grizzled head and grinned. "He pretty good at that, too."

"Yes, he's very good with his hands. I'm glad he's being a help to you, Albert. Guess I'll go see what he's up to."

"He a good boy. Just needed to know folks care."

"I know." Charles patted Albert on the back, then headed out the door. Now, what was the boy building?

He stepped through the open barn door and followed the sound of hammering to the rear of the old building behind the cow stalls.

Jeremiah glanced up. "Hi, Mr. Charles." His hands moved quickly as he signed. Quite an improvement lately.

"Hello, Jeremiah. Just saw Albert. He says you're a great worker and a good boy."

His lips turned up on one side. "Yeah, I like Albert, too. He's teaching me a lot."

Well, that was definitely an improvement on the boy who thought he already knew everything. Except signing and lip-reading in the beginning. But, to be honest, Jeremiah was proving to be a fast learner with those things, too.

"What are you building now?" It appeared to be some sort of stool.

Jeremiah ducked his head, but not before Charles saw the sheepish grin that appeared on his face. "Trying to make something to help the shorter girls get on the horses easier." He spoke in his stumbling speech, and with his head down, Charles had to listen closely to make out the words.

Charles glanced at the boy in surprise. Did this have something to do with this afternoon's teasing?

"That's very nice of you. Did Miss Livvy ask you to?"

Jeremiah leaned back on his heels and appeared to be in thought for a moment. "Well, yes and no."

"I see. Well, it's very nice of you and I'm sure Miss Olivia and the girls will be grateful."

"I guess." He returned to his project and, appearing satisfied, he picked up a piece of sandpaper and started sanding. "I figure this is big enough to set safely on the mounting block, don't you?"

Charles stooped and eyed the stool-like structure. It had a broad base, and one step to climb to the top, which was also broad and smooth. Wasn't a very pretty sight, but it appeared solid and serviceable.

"Yes, I believe this will work fine." He stood and brushed his hands off. "Of course we'd better try it out before you hand it over to the ladies."

Jeremiah gave him a disgusted look and signed furiously. "Well, of course. I wouldn't give it to them unless I knew it was safe."

"Of course not. I didn't mean to imply that." Charles signed back.

"Oh." Jeremiah grinned.

"Supper will be ready in less than an hour. Don't stay out here much longer."

The aroma of Selma's cloves, ham and candied yams greeted Charles as he stepped into the foyer. Selma always put cloves in her ham. A couple of times he'd been the recipient of one she'd forgotten to remove, but it was well worth it. He'd never tasted better ham anywhere. He smiled. But Livvy's ma's was a close second.

He went up to change into fresh clothing before supper. When he came down, Trent had just stepped into the foyer.

"Charles. Just the man I was hoping to see."

"What can I do for you, my friend?"

Trent removed a light coat and hung it on the hall tree.

"A coat?"

"The temperature seems to have dropped a few degrees in the past half hour or so. Thought I'd bring it along."

"I hope it brings some rain with it." The threat of fires hung over them daily and the woods behind the school were a deadly reminder.

Trent shook his head. "Not a cloud in the sky."

"I heard from Frank Saunders's lawyer. He's willing to go out to the farm and confront the brother, but not alone. Was wondering if you could get away this weekend and go along with me?"

"I'd love the opportunity to see that scoundrel's face when he realizes he's been found out." And Charles would have a few words for the bully about his treatment of Jeremiah and his mother.

"I thought we could take the train out late Friday afternoon. But we probably won't make it back for church Sunday."

Charles groaned inwardly. He wouldn't get to see Livvy. Maybe he could take a ride over after supper tonight to let her know.

"Friday will be fine. We have to get this matter taken care of as soon as possible."

Despite objections voiced by Charles and Trent, Mrs. Saunders insisted on going with them to the farm.

"After all, the property belongs to my son and me. I

need to be there in case there is a legal matter to be decided."

Charles, deferring to Trent, glanced in his direction.

Trent nodded. "Your attorney will be waiting for us at the hotel in Rome. He plans to get a law enforcement officer to go with us to confront your brother-in-law."

Relief washed over her face as she gave a quick nod. "And if the law refuses to get involved?"

"I don't really see how they can, under the circumstances, but if they do refuse, you will need to wait for us at the hotel."

She opened her mouth as though to argue the matter, then suddenly acquiesced. "Very well, Dr. Quincy. I can see the wisdom in that."

Charles's sigh of relief echoed Trent's as they said farewell to Mrs. Saunders and left.

On Friday afternoon, a sense of anticipation ran through Charles as the three of them boarded the train.

He listened to the chug of the engine as it pulled out of the station, but in his mind's eye he was seeing his fist explode into Edward Saunders's face. Shock ran through him as he straightened in his seat and glanced around, a sick feeling in the pit of his stomach.

He'd never been a violent man. In fact, he had no patience with those who were, like Saunders. Of course he was upset over the injustice and cruelty heaped upon Jeremiah and his mother. But physical violence wasn't the answer.

Father, forgive me and please deliver me from this anger. He waited, expecting instant peace to flow over him, but the anger remained, like a rattlesnake coiled in the pit of his stomach, poised to strike.

He scooted down in the seat and tried to sleep, but sleep eluded him. Sighing, he reached into his satchel and retrieved a notebook. He worked on class assignments until the train pulled into the station at Rome.

They walked the half block to the hotel and signed in. Mrs. Saunders immediately went to her room to freshen up and change. Charles and Trent took their single bags to their room and came back down. Upon inquiring, they found Mr. Dade, the lawyer, having an early dinner in the immaculate dining room. He invited them to join him at his table.

Charles and Trent both ordered coffee, but waited for Mrs. Saunders to come down before they ordered dinner.

The dinner conversation with Mr. Dade was more than satisfactory. He said Saunders had no legal claim to the farm whatsoever and the man would do well to gather his gear and leave without a fuss. A deputy would accompany them to the farm after dinner.

After the meal, Mrs. Saunders rode with Mr. Dade in his buggy while Charles and Trent rented horses from the livery stable.

Accompanied by Jess Williams, the deputy, they pulled into the farmyard just after darkness had fallen. A lamp burned in the cabin window.

They stepped onto the porch and Mr. Dade lifted his hand to knock, but Mrs. Saunders stepped forward.

"That's not necessary, Mr. Dade. After all, this is my home." She turned the knob and pushed open the door.

A short, balding man jumped to his feet. "Faith!" He glanced around at the men with her. A look of fear crossed his face, quickly replaced by cunning. "I've been worried sick. Where did you disappear to?"

Faith Saunders planted her hands on her narrow hips and glared at him. "A better question is why did you lie to me, Ed?"

"About what, sis?"

"I'm not your sister and you know what you lied about. Mr. Dade is Frank's lawyer. He has the will leaving the farm and everything else to me and Jeremiah. You lied."

"Aw, Faith. I was just teasing you. I was gonna tell you the truth soon. And wouldn't you have been happy?"

"I don't believe you, Ed. I'd also like to know what you did with the gold and the cash you stole from me."

His face went ashen. "Hey, I didn't steal nothing. I was using that money for supplies and stuff."

"Well, hand the rest over."

"There ain't nothing more left."

"Ma'am, if this man stole from you, you can press charges and I'll lock him up."

Faith looked at the deputy, then back to Ed. "No. I just want him out of my house and off my property."

Wasn't she going to mention him beating Jeremiah? Charles stepped forward. "There's also another matter."

"Who are you? And what lies have you hatched up to add to my sister-in-law's?"

Charles felt that anger rise up again and he wanted to smash his fist into the sneering face. *Forgive me, Lord, and help me, please.* He turned to the sheriff. "He's been beating his nephew for over four years, since the boy was nine years old."

The deputy frowned. "Do you have proof?"

"Scars all over the boy's back and shoulders. It's bad. Very bad."

"There's nothing I can do until I see some proof. If you'll bring the boy and let me see him and talk to him, maybe I can throw this thief in the hoosegow. Maybe not. Depends on the proof."

"But he'll be long gone by then," Charles protested.

"Sorry. But don't worry. You get me that proof and I'll find him."

"It's lies. All of it. I didn't beat anyone. Tell them, Faith."

"Why would you expect me to lie for you, Ed? You abused my son, you hit me over and over again, and you tried to steal our property. I want you to get your things and leave, right now, or I will press charges against you for stealing from me."

Ten minutes later, they watched him ride away. Charles sighed. Would the man ever be brought to justice?

Chapter 14

Livvy arrived at the school on Monday afternoon. She'd scheduled the extra riding day because Charles would be back from Rome and she was breathless with curiosity about what had happened there. But the girls had also been asking for two days a week instead of one and P.H. had given Livvy permission, as long as the girls kept up their grades.

She found Charles in the science room, grading papers. He rose with a cry of pleasure and reached for her hands. "Livvy. I was about to ride over to the parsonage, but I heard the girls talking about today's riding lesson."

"Yes, sorry to search you out. You're obviously busy, but I have a few minutes and couldn't wait any longer to hear about the Saunders farm."

"Everything went well." He led Livvy to a chair and then told her everything that had happened at Severn's Flat.

"Oh, that's wonderful. But they still haven't locked up

that evil man for what he did to Jeremiah and Faith." She frowned and bit her lip.

"No, but Trent and I are taking Jeremiah and his mother to Rome one day this week. Trent has to check on his patients first and make sure everyone is taken care of. Once the authorities see the boy's scars and hear his story, I'm sure they'll put Saunders behind bars."

"I certainly hope so. The thought of that man running loose gives me chills. What if he comes after Jeremiah?"

"If you'd seen the panic on the man's face, you wouldn't worry. He's long gone by now. But the sheriff and deputy will find him. Never fear."

Livvy stood and smiled. "If you believe it that strongly, then I'll believe, too. And now I'd better get to the stable where the girls are no doubt waiting for me."

He winked and grinned. "I'll see you later."

With a wave of her fingers, she stepped out of the room and headed downstairs, lighthearted and blushing from the wink. If Charles wasn't interested in her romantically, he must be losing his mind.

The girls ran to meet her, laughing with excitement. Molly grabbed Livvy's hand. "Thanks for giving us this extra day, Miss Livvy."

"It's my pleasure, Molly." To her surprise, she found that her statement was true. No twinge of fear upset her joy today. "I see you have the horses ready. Who's first today?"

"Lily Ann." Margaret smiled and placed her hand on the little girl's back. "Come on, I'll help you mount."

They stepped over to the mounting block and Margaret took the tiny girl's hand.

"Wait!" Jeremiah came from the barn carrying an odd-looking contraption. As he drew near, Livvy saw that it was some sort of stool or table.

Suspicious that he was up to more of his tricks, she

watched carefully as he set it solidly on the mounting block.

"Here, Lily Ann. Feel this so you'll understand where to put your feet."

The little girl reached out trustingly and examined the new stool. Her hand found the step then moved smoothly over the flat top. "Why it's to help me mount. Thank you, Jeremiah." She was careful to look directly at him as she spoke.

"It's nothing," Jeremiah mumbled as he took her hand and helped her onto the mounting block.

"I can do the rest by myself."

He grinned and removed his hand but stood close as she climbed to the wide top of the stool. She paused and took a deep breath, then put her left foot into the stirrup that hung down from the extra pommel. In no time she pulled herself up and into the sidesaddle. A huge smile lit up her face.

Livvy stepped over, adjusted the stirrup and moved Lily around a little bit on the saddle. "Perfect."

She turned to Jeremiah. "That was a very nice thing to do for the girls, Jeremiah."

"Aww. It wasn't much," he signed. "Mr. Charles and I checked it out to make sure it's safe. You don't need to worry about it falling off as long as you set it on the block straight."

With a chorus of thanks from the girls, Jeremiah's face turned red. He waved and walked away toward the barn.

What a transformation this act of kindness had made in Jeremiah. Who would have thought it?

When the lesson was over and the girls had run inside, chattering with excitement, Livvy asked Albert to bring her buggy around. Instead, Jeremiah came out leading the horse and rig.

"Thanks, Jeremiah."

"It's nothing," he stammered and then switched to signs. "I wanted to tell you how sorry I am for teasing the girls before. I don't know why I did it. But I'm sorry."

"I know you are, dear. You apologized when you went to all the trouble to make the new stool and give it to them. And now you've apologized verbally."

"I told Brenda I was sorry, too. I think she forgave me."

"I'm sure she did. And I forgive you. And I know God does, too. So I don't think you need to worry about it anymore."

A quiet joy shone on the boy's face, softening the hard edges of his jaw.

"Well, I'll see you at church Sunday, Miss Livvy."

"And I'll be looking forward to seeing you there." Livvy smiled and climbed into the buggy, then drove away.

As she rounded the drive by the house, she found Charles waiting. "Would it be all right if I come over later?"

"Actually, Ma told me to invite you to supper."

"Perfect. I'll be over in a little while."

Livvy smiled and quickly drove away before he had a chance to kiss her or hug her or yank her off the buggy seat. There was no predicting what Charles would do these days. But she had to admit that, so far, she liked it.

She got home in time to freshen up, then help Ma finish supper. Charles paid plenty of compliments to the meal, which made Ma beam. Pa kept giving Charles strange looks and it was with a sense of relief that Livvy stepped outside with Charles after supper.

"Goodness. Pa was acting strange. I'm so sorry, Charles."

"I'm not offended at all. I think he's wondering what my intentions are toward his daughter." He took her hand as she stepped off the porch.

Livvy blushed and warmth slid down her body. Did Charles have intentions toward her? It certainly sounded like it. And if so, she had no doubt they were honorable. And that would mean…marriage? She hastened to change the subject rather than let her imagination run wild. "Let's walk by the river."

"Sounds good to me."

"I was so happy with Jeremiah today. He not only gave the girls the new stool, which works very well, by the way, but he apologized profusely. And he meant it."

"I believe Jeremiah has always had a good heart. It just got a little hard through the years."

"It's no wonder. He's had so much to endure. I'm glad it's over."

As they neared the river, Charles took her hand in his. Her heart sped up. *Oh, God, I think I'm going to faint.*

She took several slow breaths and soon calm was restored. Now she was conscious of his hand, strong but gentle around hers.

They walked in silence, hand in hand, until finally Charles said, "I'd better get you inside or your father will likely do more than give me 'looks.'"

Livvy giggled as Charles left her at the front door. She giggled again as he mounted his horse and rode away, then wondered why in the world she had giggled. It was the perfect ending to a perfect day. And he hadn't even kissed her.

"That's a terrible idea, Hattie." Mrs. Couch frowned at her best friend, Hattie Brown.

Livvy put her hand over her mouth and patted back a giggle. She'd been giggling an awful lot lately. Perhaps from outright happiness because there was no doubt in her mind anymore that Charles cared about her. And not just as a friend.

"Now, Vera. That was just plain rude. My idea was not terrible. Just because you don't like the idea of the young folks playing Spin the Bottle doesn't make it a bad idea."

"If we're knee-deep in snow, you might change your tune. Do you want Carrie Ann to trudge down the road in knee-deep snow?"

At that, every woman in the church exploded with laughter. "Really, Vera. When have we had more than an inch of snow? And that came after Christmas. Don't be silly."

Mrs. Couch stood, lips pressed together, and started gathering her things.

Livvy's mother jumped up and stepped over to the insulted lady. "Now, Vera. Please don't leave. You know how much we value your input at these planning events. I don't think we could plan a picnic or festival without your help. And now we also have the dance to plan for."

"I'm sorry, Vera." Mrs. Brown stepped over and put her arm around her friend. "Maybe you're right about Spin the Bottle."

Mrs. Couch's eyes softened as she looked at her friend and suddenly she laughed. "No, I'm not. You know why I hate that game."

Then both old friends laughed uproariously.

They sat side by side as Mrs. Couch told her story. "When Hattie and I were girls, I had a terrible crush on the dentist who lived in the next county. One year we had what we called a play party. Nowadays they call them square dances. And he came. When one of the games was Spin the Bottle, I was determined to get to walk down the path with Grover the dentist. But another girl won that dubious honor. She ended up marrying him and from what I heard, didn't get that great a deal. But it still stung that she got the fellow I wanted and I've always hated that game."

By now laughter had washed away the strain. Soon, to Livvy's relief, they were back to planning the Harvest Festival and Dance.

"Has anyone checked with Ezra Bines to see if we can use their old abandoned barn, as we did last time?"

"Yes, Reverend Shepherd spoke to him last week. He also agreed to barbecue if Selma will part with her sauce again."

Livvy spoke up. "I'm sure she will, as long as no one tries to get the recipe from her. That was Virgie's original recipe. She passed it on when she turned the kitchen over to Selma."

"The best sauce I've ever eaten." Actually, now that Livvy thought about it, other than her mother's, it was the only barbecue sauce she'd ever eaten. She shot a quick glance at her mother and met her laughing eyes. She'd been caught, but Ma was a good sport.

Ma quickly spoke up. "And Selma has already promised jars of her canned jellies and preserves for the booths."

Everyone began to chime in with details of their donations. The proceeds from all sales at the Harvest Festival always went to help the poor in the area for Christmas and the upcoming winter months. This year a couple of families, displaced by the fires, would need most of it.

"By the way, Livvy. I know we are off the subject of young love, but I've noticed a certain young man paying you a lot of extra attention lately. And he definitely has a gleam in his eye." Mrs. Couch smiled, not unkindly, in Livvy's direction.

Livvy's face burned. Oh, dear. She hadn't realized that people had noticed. She wasn't sure whether to be glad or sorry. And how should she reply?

"I, for one, think he would be a nice catch," Mrs. Brown

said. "He's a gentleman. He's able to provide for a wife and he's very kind. Look at what he's doing for Jeremiah."

"Well, Dr. Trent is helping, too." Livvy glanced at Abigail.

Abigail smiled her thanks. "Yes, but Trent wouldn't have known unless Charles brought it to his attention and Charles is right by his side at every turn."

Livvy nodded, glad the subject had turned a little. "Yes. In fact, Charles and Trent are leaving for Rome again next week with Jeremiah and his mother to testify against the scoundrel who hurt Jeremiah and tried to steal their property. Everyone pray that he's kept in jail where he belongs this time."

"Perhaps we should also pray for that man's soul, Livvy." Ma bit her lip and gave her daughter a worried look.

"Yes, ma'am. Of course, we should." *I'm sorry, Lord. I hadn't even thought to pray for that man. I'm so angry with him I didn't even see the need. Please soften my heart.*

"And now, I think we'd do best to get back to our planning. Have we decided on a theme for the dance?"

"I thought we should have a square dance." Carrie Ann Brown glanced at her mother, who frowned.

"No, the skirts are too short."

"Well, we could wear long ones, couldn't we?"

The subject of a square dance took up the next half hour, and then Livvy interrupted, saying, "How about a fancy dress ball?"

Carrie Ann said, "I swear, Livvy. You are getting old in your thinking. Maybe it *is* time for you to get married."

"Why, Carrie Ann." The girl's mother looked mortified. "That wasn't nice at all. Livvy is only a few years older than you."

"Sorry, Livvy."

"It's all right. And Mrs. Brown, I'm twenty-six and Carrie Ann is only nineteen. But I certainly don't believe my thinking is old. After all, Carrie Ann, with those raven locks of yours, can you imagine what you would look like in the moonlight wearing a red ball gown? Or even royal blue to match your eyes?"

Carrie's blue orbs widened at the thought. Her lips tilted in a smile. "You might be right at that, Livvy."

Ma's brow furrowed. "That might prove to be difficult. It's such a short time to make fancy ball gowns."

Mrs. Brown's face also held a frown. "I agree. Although it would be beautiful. Not enough time, though." She gave her daughter a glance full of regret.

"How about later in the year?" Ma said. "We could have our Harvest Festival in October instead of November. Then a Christmas ball in early December?"

"Yes!" Mrs. Brown breathed a sigh of relief. "That sounds like a wonderful idea."

Finally, they planned on a plain Harvest Dance with some of the numbers called as in a square dance, and some waltz-type. The booths were all planned and, except for a few odds and ends, the organizers of the Harvest Festival and Dance were ready to tackle practical matters, such as cleaning and decorating.

Livvy, afraid the subject of Charles might be brought up again, breathed a sigh of relief when the last lady walked out the door.

"Whew."

Ma chuckled. "I think we're all a little curious about you and Charles. And I'm more than curious. Anything to tell, daughter?"

"Not yet, Ma. But when there is, you'll be the first to know."

Chapter 15

Charles winced as Jeremiah, seated across from him, cracked his knuckles again. The boy was obviously a bundle of nerves and Charles had no idea how to help him.

Mrs. Saunders patted her son's restless fingers. At once, his hands stilled. Charles smiled. Amazing, the power of a mother.

The train whistle blared, then softened to a mournful howl as they rounded a curve.

Within a few minutes they pulled into the station at Rome.

After disembarking, Jeremiah shouldered his mother's suitcase and his own small bag. By the time they'd registered at the hotel and stashed their luggage, it was dinnertime.

Charles grinned as Jeremiah's glance darted his way. The boy gazed around the dining room at the scurrying waiters, the gleaming table appointments and the high-domed trays. But as soon as his fried chicken dinner arrived, his appetite superseded the sparkle and shine and he dug in with gusto.

Afterward, Mrs. Saunders went to her room while Trent and Charles took Jeremiah around to a local carnival. The boy might as well have a little fun before the trying day ahead.

The chill wind whipped through Charles's light jacket as they strolled to the outskirts of town where the carnival was in progress. He was happy that Jeremiah's mother had seen to it that her son's jacket was heavy and warm.

Jeremiah was immediately drawn to a small arena where a makeshift rodeo was being held. The boy's eyes gleamed as, one after another, all the cowboys were thrown.

"I could have stayed on," he boasted as they made their way back through the crowds to the hotel.

Charles eyed him. Should he nip the boasting in the bud or let it be?

Trent clapped Jeremiah on the shoulder. "You know, I think maybe you could have."

Jeremiah's face glowed and his shoulders straightened.

Charles glanced at Trent. Another wise lesson learned from his friend. Pride in one's accomplishments wasn't so bad for a boy. It lifted his confidence. And that was something Jeremiah desperately needed.

The next morning, after breakfast, they walked to the sheriff's office to meet with the judge who'd been appointed to hear the case.

The office was neat and fairly clean, although the smell of pipe and cigar smoke hung heavily on the air.

The sheriff leaned back in a chair with his feet on the desk. When Mrs. Saunders stepped into the room, he jerked his legs off the desk and stood. "Mrs. Saunders?"

"Yes, I'm Faith Saunders and this is my son, Jeremiah. I believe you've met Dr. Quincy and Mr. Waverly."

The sheriff nodded to acknowledge Charles and Trent, then turned back to Mrs. Saunders. "The judge is waiting for you and your son in back. It'll be more private there."

"I'd like for Dr. Quincy and Mr. Waverly to be present, as well." Her hand shook as she motioned toward them.

The sheriff shook his head. "Were they witness to the alleged beatings?"

Mrs. Saunders's face flamed. "Alleged?"

"Sorry, ma'am. We have to call it that until his guilt is proven."

"I understand." Her voice trembled, but she cleared her throat. "No, they were not witnesses to the beatings, Sheriff. But Dr. Quincy has examined my son thoroughly and Mr. Waverly is his trusted teacher."

The sheriff scratched his ear. "I dunno. Maybe the doctor, but I doubt Waverly's getting in."

Charles laid his hand on her arm. "It's all right. I'll wait here."

"But Jeremiah might need you." She turned to the sheriff with pleading eyes. "Will you at least ask?"

The sheriff took a deep breath. "All right. I'll ask." He headed down a short hall. In a few minutes, he was back.

"Judge says all of you can come on back. He's ready to hear the case. He's going to wait until after your testimony before he brings in the prisoner."

Charles brought up the rear as they all filed down the hall and passed through the door the sheriff indicated. A portly man sat behind a scarred desk. He glanced up from a stack of papers.

"Hmm. Yes." He looked over his glasses. "Mrs. Saunders, please take a chair. I'm Judge Beamer." He glanced at the sheriff.

"Your honor, this is Dr. Quincy, who's been treating the boy, and this gentleman is his teacher, Charles Waverly, his, uh, translator."

"Mrs. Saunders, I see you've given written testimony. Would you repeat that to me, please?"

"Yes, sir." She told their story, beginning with her husband's death and her brother-in-law's arrival at the farm. When she told of the beatings, her tears prevented her from speaking for several minutes.

"Take your time." The judge's eyes were kind, although he tapped impatiently on the desk.

She blotted her eyes. "I can continue." When she'd finished the story, ending with their confrontation with Ed Saunders, the judge stood.

"Jeremiah, would you mind showing me your scars, please?" When Charles signed the request, the boy complied. Judge Beamer stared intently at the back and shoulders that had been so abused.

Finally, he turned to Trent. "Dr. Quincy, could you explain these markings for me?"

"Yes, Your Honor, I can." Trent pointed out old scars that had been on Jeremiah's body for several years. Then fresher ones from only months before. "As you can tell from the depth of these ridges, the lacerations cut in deeply."

The judge clamped his lips together and fury filled his eyes. "Jeremiah, would you mind leaving your shirt off while I call in the accused?" When Jeremiah didn't answer, the judge sent a silent plea to Charles who stepped over and signed to Jeremiah.

For a moment, fear jumped into Jeremiah's eyes. He glanced at Charles, who gave him a smile and a nod. "All right. I'll leave it off."

When the deputy brought Ed Saunders into the room in

handcuffs, the first thing the prisoner saw was his nephew with bared back. His face blanched. "I didn't do that!"

"Who did, then?" the judge retorted. "His mother?"

"I don't know who did it. Maybe my brother."

"Don't you dare accuse Frank of something so heinous." Mrs. Saunders lurched forward, fury in her eyes, but the judge stepped between her and her brother-in-law.

"I've seen enough. The prisoner is to be held over at the county jail in Atlanta until trial. And I'm the one hearing the case."

He walked out, giving Jeremiah a nod and his mother a wink.

The deputy took Saunders back to his cell to prepare for transport to Atlanta and Jeremiah gave a whoop. "Does this mean Uncle Ed's going to prison?"

Trent grinned. "Well, with Judge Beamer officiating I don't think he can possibly avoid it."

"Can we go see the farm before we go back to school?" Jeremiah sent a pleading glance to his mother.

She smiled and hugged him. "If Dr. Trent and Charles don't mind, I'd love to."

"Do you think the farm's all right, Ma?"

"Of course. Mr. Thomas has been watching the place. I also asked him to find a hired hand for us."

"You did?" Jeremiah gave his mom a look of respect.

"Well, yes. This is our property, son. We have to take care of it."

"Are we going to live there again?"

"I thought I'd keep working for Patrick and Helen until you break for Christmas, then we'll spend Christmas on the farm. Does that sound all right to you?"

"Yes, ma'am, it does. What about after Christmas?"

"Well, after Christmas you will need to go back to school, Jeremiah. Now that you're going to be a man of property, you'll need a good education. And you also need to learn to speak and sign better. Right?"

Jeremiah nodded. "Right."

A twinge of sadness bit at Charles at Jeremiah's expression, but he'd be all right. It wasn't easy for the children to leave parents and home, but the alternative of no education was much worse.

They found the cabin and property much as they'd left it. The two cows and the mules were taken care of and had plenty of hay in their stalls. Chickens ran freely across the yard.

Mrs. Saunders left a few things from her suitcase and retrieved some others.

Charles glanced at Jeremiah, who stood beside the fireplace, looking at a photograph on the mantelpiece. Mrs. Saunders stepped over, placed an arm around her son and they gazed at the picture of her husband and his father.

A pensiveness hung in the air as they drove away from the farm, but by the time they boarded the train and settled into their seats, cheerfulness had returned, as Jeremiah and his mother talked about the farm, and they rode back to Magnolia Junction with an almost holiday air.

"Livvy, what are you doing?" Ma's voice rang out in surprise as she stood on the porch, gazing up at Livvy on Henry's back.

Livvy glanced back. "Riding Henry over to the school."

"That's wonderful." Ma beamed and waved.

Livvy grinned and urged Henry forward. The change had been gradual, but little by little, she'd lost the fear that had hounded her since she was seven years old.

The crisp November air nipped at her cheeks and, by the time she arrived at the school, she was ready for candied apples and hot apple cider. She grinned. She'd need to wait for the Harvest Festival for the candied apples, but maybe she'd go to the kitchen and coax a cup of cider out of Selma before the riding lesson.

Lily Ann and Molly came running to meet her as she dismounted. "You rode a horse over." Molly's exclamation rang out.

Lily held a hand out and giggled when Henry sniffed her fingers. "What's his name?"

"Henry, and he loves apples. Maybe you could give him a slice or two after the lesson."

"How about now?" Lily Ann jumped up and down.

Livvy laughed and tickled the little girl's ribs. "Not now. Let's go see if we can talk Selma into giving us something hot to drink."

"Cook makes the bestest hot chocolate in the world." She turned and signed to Molly the words she'd just spoken.

Molly laughed and nodded. "Yes, she does." Molly's speech was much better now that Helen was working with her at home.

The girls each grabbed one of Livvy's hands and swung them as they walked to the kitchen.

Selma came scurrying as they walked in. "You chilrun get on out of here now. I'm trying to get dinner ready."

Livvy laughed. "Sorry. I'm afraid it's my fault. I'm quite cold after my ride over and planned to beg you for something hot to drink. But I see you're very busy, so we'll just get on out of your hair."

"No, you won't." Selma motioned to a small table by the wall. "You three sit yourselves right down there and I'll get you some cider."

"Oh, that sounds wonderful. If you're sure."

"And I guess you two would rather have some hot chocolate." Both girls nodded enthusiastically.

With their tummies warm from the hot drinks, Livvy

and the two girls went back to the stable where the other girls were waiting.

Livvy waited until Elizabeth and Margaret mounted their horses, then she climbed on Henry's back. "All right, girls, we'll ride straight across to the other side of the woods, then down the riverbank to the old live oak, and back again."

"Can we race to the live oak?" Margaret, always competitive, grinned with excitement.

"Not yet, Margaret. Most of the girls aren't ready for racing. Remember, they haven't been riding for as long as you have."

Margaret simpered, then her nose curled. "Eww, something's burning."

"Girls, stop!" Anxiety surged through Livvy. What if their woods were burning? "Wait here. Don't move. I'll be right back."

Urging Henry forward, she fought against his head. Was he being contrary because of the woods or was it fire? But there was no smoke in the air.

She came to the edge of the woods and pulled up. The foliage on the edge of the far side of the river was smoldering. She whirled Henry around and rode back as fast as she could through the woods to where the girls waited. Their faces were pale and anxious.

"Let's go. Hurry. The woods across the river are burning a little. We have to get help."

She stayed close behind Elizabeth, while Margaret led the way down the well-worn path back to the school.

"Albert! Albert!" She slid off Henry's back while Margaret helped Elizabeth. The girls huddled around their friends as they all ran back to the school.

The elderly man came hobbling out from the stable.

"Fire across the river. I'm going to tell Charles and

Howard. You'd best ring the school bell so people will come."

Halfway to the house, she met P.H. and the entire staff.

P.H. nodded when she heard the bell sound its sonorous peal.

"Fast work, Livvy. Good job."

Within a few moments, wagons and horses began to pull into the schoolyard. With shovels, plows and mules, the men went around the old river road to the other side and once more did what needed to be done. Thanks to quick thinking and a fast response, within four hours the fire was completely out. Several men volunteered to watch throughout the night, to make sure no stray cinders caught fire.

After supper, P.H. held a meeting on the front porch for Dr. Trent and all the teachers, including Livvy.

"This is the closest a fire has come to the school. We can take no more chances. I hesitate to evacuate the school at this point. But until further notice, I'm canceling all riding classes and all nature walks. I don't want to see a student or a member of the staff anywhere near the woods. Except, of course, for watchmen patrolling the area for more fires breaking out."

Trent cleared his throat. "I'll call a meeting for volunteers. No one in the community wants to see the school in danger."

P.H.'s face cleared and she smiled. "I know that, Trent. The community is a great support for our school. I think it belongs to all of them as much as to the students and staff."

Livvy drew a deep breath, pleased to hear the director's comment. P.H. had only been here a couple of years and people were only recently starting to warm up to her. Not that she was snobbish, just a little more reticent in public than the folks around the community were used to.

Livvy leaned back in her chair and glanced at Charles, who returned her smile.

He leaned forward and whispered in her ear, "P.H. is a good old girl at heart. Just a little hard to get to know sometimes."

How did he always seem to read her mind?

As Livvy rode home, her heartfelt prayer was that the rains would begin soon and no one would be hurt or have their homes destroyed by more fires.

Chapter 16

"Here now! That wasn't nice, Joe Ramsey." Livvy frowned at the overall-clad young man who leaned against a ladder.

Joe gave the ladder another small shake. The eldest Bines girl, nearly to the top, squealed in terror. Or, at least, she sounded terrified to Livvy. But from the grin on the girl's face, maybe not.

The young people either didn't hear Livvy, or they ignored her. She shrugged and carried a box full of pinecones and autumn leaves to Carrie Ann, who was supposed to be decorating the back wall. But just now, she was gazing wide-eyed up at Clark Bell who grinned down at her from his towering height.

Livvy sighed. Young love, everywhere she looked. Was she destined to miss out on that part of life? Surely not. Surely Charles would declare himself anytime now. But what if he didn't? What if she'd just imagined his interest?

She blinked back the sudden tears that sprang to her eyes. In that case, she'd have to settle for being single forever. She couldn't, in good conscience, marry someone else, when she would always love Charles.

The barn door swung open and Charles sauntered in carrying three boxes, stacked one on top of the other. Livvy blotted her eyes. Had he seen her tears? She stuffed the handkerchief into her sleeve.

A moment later, Charles was at her side. "Livvy, where should I put these jars? They're an additional, last-minute offering from Selma."

"Oh, spiced apples and plum preserves. We don't have any of those yet." She motioned toward the middle of the room, where two tables were quickly filling up. "Put them over there for now. We're going to sort them all out later."

He carried the boxes over and deposited them on one of the tables, but was back in a hurry. "Hey, you've been crying."

"I think I got smoke in my eyes."

He ran a thumb over her cheek, a glance of concern scanning her face. "Are you sure? Has someone said something to hurt your feelings?"

"No, no, I'm fine, Charles. I promise." And it was true, for suddenly the world seemed bright again. Charles was here. And he cared.

While Charles went to help some of the other men build a stage for the musicians and the dance caller, Livvy left the decorating to the young people and helped sort out the jars of donated foodstuffs.

The promised pies and other baked goods would be brought fresh in two weeks, on the day of the festival. A shiver slid down Livvy's skin. She'd always loved parties and dances, but this one held a promise and hope she hadn't experienced before. She felt it deep inside her. Something wonderful was going to happen.

Mrs. Brown set a jar of spiced peaches in a group of the same and nudged Mrs. Couch. "Told you he was sweet on her."

Mrs. Couch gave a little laugh and glanced at Livvy. "It's no use, dear. We can see with our own eyes. That young man is befuddled. He'll be down on his knees, asking that important question, before long."

"Yes." Mrs. Brown put her hands on her hips and gave Livvy a serious look. "I certainly hope you don't turn this one down as you did all the others, Miss Picky. You're not getting any younger, you know."

"Mama!" Carrie Ann's horrified exclamation rang in Livvy's ears.

But Livvy was already halfway to the doors. That woman was getting more and more insufferable.

Livvy charged out the barn door and hurried around to the side of the building, where she fell against the wall. Angry tears rushed down her cheeks. Must that woman always humiliate her? There was no telling how many people overheard her remark. Certainly Carrie Ann had.

The barn door creaked and Livvy stood still, hoping no one would see her.

"Livvy, where are you?" Charles's quiet call reached her ears.

Oh, no. He must have heard Hattie Brown. She couldn't face him, now. She simply wouldn't answer.

Charles came around the corner and took her hands. "Hey, what are you doing, hiding out here? Those kids are getting a little rowdy in there. I can't say I blame you." He grinned and squeezed her hands.

Maybe he hadn't heard, after all. Livvy took a deep breath.

Charles reached out and smoothed a stray curl from her brow. "How about I tie the horse to the back of your buggy and you and I go for a drive. Then I'll take you home."

"That sounds wonderful." She darted a glance toward the barn. "But I have to gather up Mama's baskets first."

"I'll help. Come on." Hand in hand, they walked toward the barn where he opened the door and let her pass through.

Somehow Charles managed to block everyone who made any attempt to come near her. They gathered all of Mama's things and headed out to the buggy.

"How old is the youngest Brown girl?" Charles asked out of the blue as they headed out of the Bineses' yard.

"Annie? Fifteen, I think. Why?" Annie Bines was cute as a button and one of Livvy's favorites of the younger bunch.

"She's a nuisance, that's why." Charles gave her a pained look. "The girl follows me around at every community function. What's her problem?"

Livvy giggled, remembering her own crush on her Sunday school teacher when she was Annie's age. "I think she's enamored of you, Charles."

A look of horror crossed his face. "No! How do I fix that?"

"You can't. Don't worry. It will wear off eventually. My crush on Bennett Lane did."

"And who is Bennett Lane?" His brow furrowed in mock anger.

"He was my Sunday school teacher when I was Annie's age. I was devastated when he proposed to Lucy Porter, but once I saw that it was serious, I ignored him until they moved away."

"Ah, so a young girl's love doesn't last."

"It depends on how young the girl is. If she's twenty,

it might last forever, but at fifteen, I don't think you have anything to worry about." She gave him a shy smile. After all, she was twenty when she'd fallen in love with him.

"Hmm. And how did you get so knowledgeable about these affairs of the heart?"

"Now you're teasing me. I'm not knowledgeable at all."

"Have you never been in love, Livvy? I mean really in love. Not the fifteen-year-old kind."

She grew silent, and warmth flooded her face. She simply couldn't answer him. It wouldn't do for him to know unless he cared about her, too. In this case, she hoped Mrs. Couch and Mrs. Brown were right.

A sudden burst of wind howled through the trees. Livvy shivered and drew her coat closer about her shoulders.

Charles reached over and spread the carriage blanket around her legs. "We'd better forget the ride and get you home. It feels as if it's getting colder."

"You don't think it's a norther, do you?" What her ma called a blue norther could come roaring down from the north, bringing extreme temperatures.

"I don't think so. It's early for that. But it's definitely getting colder." He urged the horses to a gallop and soon the church came into view.

Charles pulled around to the back door of the parsonage. "Why don't you go inside? I'll take care of your horse and buggy and head on to the school. I'll see you at church in the morning."

"Thank you, Charles. I enjoyed the ride, short as it was."

"Not as much as I did." He smiled. "Good night, Livvy." He waited until she was inside, then she glanced out the window and watched him drive over to the stable.

Only later did she realize that she hadn't thought once about her humiliation. And somehow, it seemed rather insignificant now.

* * *

Charles stepped out the front doors of Quincy School and felt a strong gust of dry wind. Worry tightened his stomach. If this continued, any fires that started would be very difficult to put out.

When the winds had come up two nights before, the night he'd driven Livvy home from the Bineses' house, he'd hoped they'd bring rain, but the only clouds in the sky were soft and billowy. And the wind showed no sign of letting up.

He turned, intending to go back inside, but the sound of horses' hooves stopped him. Trent came around the bend and drew up at the front porch.

Charles grinned. "You'd best get your horse in the stable and come inside. You're just in time for lunch."

"No, I need to get home to Abigail and the baby. I just dropped by to let you know I received a letter with the trial date. You and Mrs. Saunders will more than likely get one, too, if you haven't already, since we all have to testify."

"All right. That's good news. When is the trial?"

"They must have rushed it. It's set for three weeks from today on November 27th."

He waved a quick goodbye, then whirled his horse around and took off down the lane.

Charles stared after him. The lucky guy, to have someone to hurry home to. A vision of Livvy, holding a small child in her arms, sent a jolt through him. Should he tell her he loved her? And if he did, would she believe him?

It had been a year or less since he'd cried in her arms because Helen preferred another man. How could he tell Livvy it had only taken a few days for him to realize that what he'd felt for Helen wasn't love? She'd think he was unstable as far as women were concerned.

All he knew was that his heart longed for Livvy in a

way he'd never known was possible and the thought of living without her was almost unbearable. His best friend. His heart's love.

Lord, give me wisdom. If it is Your will for Livvy and me to marry, please give me the words to say to her. And please help her know she loves me, too. Because I know she does, Lord. We've just been friends for so long, she might not realize it. In Jesus's name. Amen.

Once more, peace washed over him, and he went inside with lightness in his heart.

At the smell of Selma's chili filling the foyer and the sight of the children lined up two by two in front of the dining room for the midday meal, Charles's stomach growled. They didn't usually get chili until the weather turned cold, but Selma must have thought the high winds were a good enough reason to make the cold-weather dish. The children's eyes were bright with excitement. Anything indicating that winter was on the way brought thoughts of Christmas to their minds. Just as it had done for him when he was a child.

Abigail Quincy had put on a big Christmas program the past two years and the children vied for the parts. Most of the parents came for that, and then they took their children home with them for Christmas.

He shook his head and gave a quiet laugh. He must not be too far away from that boy he had been, since his thoughts had jumped to the holiday so readily.

But that was a ways off. They still had the Harvest Festival and Dance. Then Thanksgiving. Charles only hoped that no more fires broke out to take lives or homes.

The chili was a hit, served with cornbread and followed by apple dumplings. At the end of the meal, Selma came in and took a mock bow. The children and staff gave her a round of applause.

One more class for the day, then school was dismissed, with instructions to the children to stay inside because of the heavy wind.

Expecting trouble from the older boys with the prospect of being confined, Charles glanced at Jeremiah. He, Sonny and Tommy were deep in conversation, their fingers flying as they signed. Sonny's eyes were bright and he and Tommy had big grins on their faces. Now what was Jeremiah up to this time? Charles watched the three boys head up the stairs.

He waited until they were out of sight, then went up to the second floor in time to see their legs disappear up the third-floor stairs, where the auditorium and playroom were located.

When he arrived at the playroom door, all three boys were on their knees, with marbles surrounding them.

"Now, here are the rules of the game." With signs and his impaired speech, Jeremiah went on to explain a game that Charles had seen the older boys play. Sonny had wanted to learn the game, but until today, the older boys had run him off when they played.

He stepped through the door. When his shadow crossed the floor, three pairs of eyes looked up at him.

"Hello, boys. Playing marbles, I see."

"Yes, sir!" Sonny's eyes lit up. "Jeremiah is teaching us a new game."

"That's nice of you, Jeremiah."

Jeremiah shook his head. "I needed something to do since we can't go out."

Charles smiled. The older boy and former bully wasn't about to admit any kindness to the younger boys.

After watching for a while, satisfied that Jeremiah wasn't involved in some mischief, Charles left and went downstairs. He glanced into the back parlor. Virgie sat with her feet up and her eyes closed. Softly, he closed the door and sauntered up the hall to the larger front parlor, where he found Howard and Felicity drinking tea and laughing.

Charles had often wondered why the two house parents, one for the girls and the other for the boys, had never married. It was obvious that they cared for each other. Just as Virgie and Albert did. And yet they'd never married, either.

"Come in, Charles." Felicity picked up a cup, decorated with an English fox-hunting scene. "Here, I'll pour you some tea. It's still hot."

"Sounds good to me." Charles plopped down on a chair by the empty fireplace and stretched his booted feet onto a brown leather footstool.

"So, Charles, have you heard anything about the trial date?" Howard, who treated the boys like his own, had been so furious when he heard about Jeremiah's abuse that he'd wanted to take the next train the Severn's Flat and, as he put it, beat the tar out of the uncle.

"Yes, as a matter of fact, Trent brought word this morning. It's set for November 27th."

"Well, I just hope that skunk doesn't get off someway."

"He won't. Don't worry. The judge is very just and he's read all the testimony and seen the evidence."

The front door slammed and boots pounded into the foyer. Charles jumped up and yanked the door open to see a wild-eyed Albert. "Albert, what's wrong?"

The old man leaned over and panted before he could speak. "The church bell ringing. Couldn't make out the signal too good at first over all that howling wind. It's fire all right. Don't know where. But it's fire."

Chapter 17

Livvy shook with fear as Pa got his gear ready to help fight the latest forest fire. What if something happened to him this time? Then another thought pierced her thoughts. The children.

"But, Pa! The school is right in its path. With the wind so strong, it could jump the bank anytime."

Pa threw another plow into the wagon and tied Henry to the back. "Livvy, you are to stay here with your mother. I don't want you anywhere near the fire. If it should jump the bank, the woods would burn like twigs, as dry as they are."

"But what about the children?" And what about Charles?

"The staff at Quincy are all trained for this type of emergency. I'm sure they have an evacuation plan."

"But another pair of hands might help."

"A pair of inexperienced hands might only get in the way. Please, daughter. Don't argue with me."

"I'm sorry, Papa." Livvy stepped back as Pa and Jake

pulled away in the wagon. But her heart was in turmoil. What if she could be of use at the school? And, if not, at least she'd know if Charles was safe. She could stay out of the way. And maybe there would be something for her to do. Virgie would tell her what to do to help.

But to disobey Pa? She pressed her lips together. Pa didn't understand. After all, she wasn't a child. He'd be glad once he knew she'd been a help.

Slipping inside the house, she found her mother on her knees in the parlor. A twinge of uncertainty squeezed Livvy's stomach. Maybe it would be more helpful for her to kneel with Mama and pray.

She squared her shoulders. No. She needed to be at the school. Not wanting to interrupt her mother's prayers, she wrote a short note and left it on the kitchen table.

She threw a light coat over her dress and slipped out the front door. A heavy gust of wind rushed around the house and knocked the door from her hand, slamming it back against the house. Livvy grabbed the door and struggled until it closed, then stumbled to the barn. Inside, she gazed at Henry's empty stall. Pa had taken all the mounts except for the carriage horses. Livvy hesitated. Would she be able to handle them and the buggy in this wind?

She hit her palm against her brow. What was she thinking?

She saddled Peaches and rode out of the churchyard, fighting the horse all the way.

Peaches dashed onto the road, neighing and rearing. She wasn't used to being ridden, she wasn't used to not being paired with Blaze and she hated the wind.

Livvy yanked on the reins and jumped off Peaches's back. She cajoled and patted until she got the horse calmed, then remounted. Soon they were trotting down the road, but not without difficulty.

By alternately cajoling and snapping a whip into the air, Livvy followed the path to the school. She sighed with relief when the road to Quincy School came into view. Shortly afterward, she rode into the stable.

Jeremiah came running up to her. "Miss Livvy, what are you doing out in this weather?"

"I came to help. Where is Mr. Charles?"

"He's across the river, helping the rest of the men fight the fire." Jeremiah frowned. "I'd have gone but they wouldn't let me. Albert told me to watch over the livestock and do whatever the staff tells me to do."

"That's good, Jeremiah. I'm sure it's a comfort to the women in the house to have a man here."

His eyes lit up and he straightened his back and shoulders. "I'll do what I can to help."

"I know you will. Now I need to go find Virgie and see what I can do."

Livvy headed for the house, where the female staff members were scurrying around getting things ready. Virgie boxed up the silver and linens to be moved in case of evacuation. She didn't seem to see Livvy, so Livvy climbed the stairs and almost collided with Molly, who ran pell-mell after the cat, Nellie Sue. Lily Ann clung to her friend's arm and charged down the stairs, too.

"Girls, you shouldn't be running on the stairs." Especially with Lily Ann not being able to see.

"But, Miss Livvy." Lily Ann's eyes filled with tears. "We got to put her in her cage so she won't run away."

"Oh, I see. All right, but get off the stairs, please, before you fall and hurt yourself."

Sonny, delighted at the chase, opened the door with a mischievous grin. The girls landed on the foyer and ran for the open front door through which Nellie Sue had escaped. The boy ran after the two girls. Goodness, she'd never seen the school in such an uproar. Obviously, they could use her help. But where? Everyone seemed to have their own duties and was going about them very well. She continued up the stairs.

Felicity and Hannah Wilson were packing clothing and bedding into boxes and trunks. Several older girls were helping.

"Is there anything I can do?"

Felicity glanced around absently. "Oh, Livvy. Hello. We have everything under control. Sally May and Flora are down the hall. You could check with them."

Livvy wandered down the long hallway and found the two maids Felicity had mentioned, but they were just finishing boxing up more clothing and bedding. They lifted a box and started to squeeze through the narrow door. Flora backed into Livvy.

"Oh. 'Scuse me, Miss Livvy. Didn't even see you there."

"It's my fault, Flora. I came to help, but it seems as if I'm only in the way."

When neither of the maids bothered to deny it, Livvy headed back downstairs and out the front door.

Sonny came bolting up on the porch, fear in his eyes. "Miss Livvy!" His hands flew as he signed. "Molly and Lily Ann ran into the woods after that cat."

"No!" Terror struck at Livvy's heart. Two little girls, one blind and one deaf, in the darkening woods with winds howling and a fire just across the river? Why hadn't she gone outside with them instead of looking around uselessly for a way to help?

"Show me where they went in, Sonny."

The boy pointed, and Livvy plunged into the woods.

"Molly! Lily Ann!" Livvy could hear the hysteria in her screams. She needed to calm down and think. She needed to pray. Her breathing grew rapid as she plunged deeper into the forest.

"Molly! Lily Ann! Where are you?" Her voice seemed to echo back at her, mocking. She had to stop this before she started imagining things. She'd heard of people hallucinating when they were in moments of fear and stress.

Livvy leaned against a tree to catch her breath and suddenly a small voice cried out, "Miss Livvy? Is that you?"

Lily Ann! Livvy shoved from the tree. "Yes, Lily, where are you? Can you follow my voice?"

"I think so." The rustling of branches came closer and Livvy followed the sounds. Suddenly, Lily Ann's and Molly's tear-streaked faces appeared around a live oak tree. Livvy ran to the girls and hugged them both to her.

"Miss Livvy! The fire jumped the river. This side is burning." Terror filled Molly's voice and she forgot to sign.

"Are you sure, Molly?" Livvy looked at her directly so Molly could read her lips. She was in no shape to tackle signing right now.

"Yes, ma'am. I saw it and grabbed Lily Ann and we ran back this way as fast as we could. She heard you calling. It's a good thing she isn't deaf or we might have never found you."

The smell of smoke and the crackling of wood proved to Livvy that Molly was right. The Quincy woods were on fire.

"Come on, girls. Let's get out of here." She took each girl by the hand and started back the way they'd come. At least, she thought so. The sound of flames crackled somewhere nearby and smoke filled the air. Was she going in the right direction? *Dear God, please help us.*

A cat meowed from behind them and Nellie Sue bounded from a tree limb and into Lily Ann's arms.

"Nellie Sue. You found us." The little girl laughed with

joy at the safe return of their pet. Although Livvy wasn't sure how safe the animal would be if Livvy couldn't get her bearings and lead them home.

By now, both girls, as well as Livvy, were coughing. No matter which way they turned there was smoke. And the ever-present terrifying sound of crackling, snapping fire.

Fear grabbed Livvy like talons. A fear worse than any she'd known. And guilt. Pa was right. All she'd done was make things worse. What had she been thinking, barging into the woods without a plan? If she hadn't been there, Sonny would have told someone about the girls, someone who would have known what to do.

With the girls clinging to her dress, Livvy started forward again. These woods were full of pine trees. They'd be sure to catch on fire soon, and then it would be too late.

But the smoke was so thick that she couldn't see. Maybe they were moving closer to the river.

What if they should die out here? It would be her fault and she could never, ever say *I'm sorry* to their parents. She could never ask Pa and Mama for forgiveness for being so foolish. She stood holding precious Lily Ann and equally precious Molly. She wanted to say, "Forgive me for causing your death."

But hadn't Abigail told her that Lily Ann had an incredible sense of direction?

"Lily Ann, do you know which way we need to go?"

The little girl paused a moment and grew still. Then she began coughing.

"I'm sorry, Miss Livvy. I can't think." She felt a tug on her sleeve and looked down to see Lily Ann's sightless eyes staring in her direction. "We need to pray now. God will take care of us."

Livvy drew in a gasp of breath, and with it she drew in

hope. "All right, Lily." She turned to Molly, but Lily was already signing to her. They all three bowed their heads.

Lily's sweet voice piped up confidently. "Dear Father in Heaven, we know You are right here watching over us, just like Reverend Shepherd always says You are. And You know how to get us out of here. So, we ask You in the name of our Sweet Jesus to help us now. Thank You. And Amen."

A loud crashing to their left resounded in the air and Jeremiah appeared, leading one of their carriage horses.

"Miss Livvy. I didn't think I'd ever find you. Come on We need to get out of here before we can't find our way back."

The trip back to the school was both harrowing and joyful. Livvy was exuberant at seeing such a quick answer to Lily Ann's prayer. The girls sat on the horse's back with the cat cradled in Lily Ann's arms.

Livvy held one side of the horse's bridle and Jeremiah the other. "How did you know we were in the woods, Jeremiah?"

"Sonny told me. I was afraid I wouldn't have time to find you, but I grabbed a horse from the stable and told Sonny to tell Virgie so she could get the word out." He glanced backward. "Wish we had something wet to put over their faces. I was afraid I wouldn't find you in time."

Livvy removed her light coat. Spreading it over the girls, she made sure their heads were loosely covered.

A scream from a tree revealed a bobcat and Jeremiah had to hold on tight to keep the horse from rearing. The bobcat jumped to another tree and disappeared.

Livvy trembled. *I won't be afraid. God sent Jeremiah just at the right time. He's going to save us from this. Thank You, Lord. And please make my faith stronger.*

The smoke seemed to be clearing a little. Maybe the fire wasn't as close as she thought.

"Jeremiah, do you know where the fire is?"

"Last I heard it was on the bank of the river. The men were plowing to try to keep it from getting any farther into Quincy's woods."

But she'd heard the crackle and popping of flames. Could those sounds have come from the riverbank? If they did, then as bad as things seemed for a while, they could have been much worse.

A horse and rider appeared, as if out of nowhere. At the sight of Charles bounding off the horse, Livvy's knees almost buckled with relief.

"Livvy!" He ran to her and gathered her into his arms, kissing her on her head. "Are you all right?"

"Yes, I'm fine."

"And the girls?" He passed his eyes over the huddled figures.

"We're all fine. Thanks to Jeremiah. He saved us."

"No, Miss Livvy," Lily Ann said. "Jesus saved us. But he used Jeremiah to do it."

"You're absolutely right, Lily Ann. Don't ever let me forget that."

Charles insisted on lifting Livvy onto his horse and he walked beside it, making sure it didn't get out of control.

Within a few minutes, they rode out of the woods to the welcome sight of Quincy School.

"I need to get back and help put the fire out. I'll tell your father that you're all right."

"You mean you came here because of me? But how did you know?"

"One of the Taylor boys rode by here to check on his farm and Virgie told him what was going on."

Livvy nodded. "I see. I'd better take the girls inside to

Felicity and then get home and let my mother know I'm all right. There doesn't seem to be anything for me to do here anyway."

Once again, recriminations overwhelmed her. Because of her disobedience, she'd put two little girls and Jeremiah in danger, and she'd caused Charles to leave the work of putting the fire out.

She drove home, wondering what her mother would have to say about her defiance. She was nearly home before it occurred to her that the wind had died down. Had it been that way when she'd left Quincy School? She'd been so tense, she couldn't remember.

She rode into the barn and took care of Peaches, brushing her down carefully. "You did a good job, girl, and you deserve a little extra hay tonight. And maybe an apple."

She gave the horse a final pat, and left her and Blaze nibbling on their apples. Surprised that her mother hadn't come out to the barn to check on her, she walked slowly to the house and went inside.

The house was silent. Livvy went to the kitchen and found her note folded as she'd left it. Startled, she rushed into the parlor to check on Ma.

Ma was kneeling just as she had been when Livvy left home nearly two hours earlier. Had she been on her knees all this time? It wouldn't be the first time. Her softly murmured prayers reached Livvy's ears. "And Father, after the fire is out and everyone is safe, please grant everyone a peaceful night's rest so they can do their day's work tomorrow. Father, I thank You once more for my wonderful husband and our precious daughter. I thank You for always looking out for us in all we do. And thank You, Lord, that because of You, we need have no fear. Father, increase my faith. In the name of Your son, Jesus. Amen."

Livvy tiptoed over and knelt by her mother, tears rolling

down her cheeks. She should have known that Mama was praying. *Thank You, Lord, for the two sincerest prayers I've ever heard. Lily Ann's and Mama's.*

Mama took her hand. "Livvy, dear. Have you been here beside me all this time?" She sniffed. "You smell like smoke. Is the stove acting up?"

"No, Mama, I haven't been here but a minute. But I wish I had been. Let me put on the kettle for tea. I need to tell you something."

Chapter 18

Charles held out his ticket to the conductor as the man walked toward them, his lips pursed in a smile and his hat perched on his head, perfectly straight.

"Thank you, sir." He punched the ticket, then proceeded to Trent and Mrs. Saunders.

"Say, Ma." Jeremiah's voice was higher than usual in his excitement, and his hands signed double time. "Do you think I could go talk with the engineer? And see what goes on up that way? Maybe even see the coal car?"

It was no wonder the boy was excited. Court day had finally arrived. Soon it would be over with and Jeremiah and his mother could get on with their lives.

Mrs. Saunders frowned and signed back slowly. "Jeremiah, slow down. I don't know what you said."

Jeremiah repeated himself, slowly this time, then gave his mother an expectant glance.

"I don't think so, son. I doubt they need or want passengers getting in their way while they do their work."

"But, Ma, I've been thinking. I really like trains. Maybe I'd rather work on a railroad someday instead of being a farmer." His hands signed as he spoke in his high voice.

The conductor's eyes twinkled. "Now, sometimes they do allow passengers with a good reason to view their work. And I'd say a possible future employee would be a good reason. Of course, you'd need to wait until the train has stopped. And you'll need your ma's permission and your father would need to go along." He nodded toward Charles.

Jeremiah, who'd watched the man's lips closely, glanced at Charles with a grin.

Mrs. Saunders blushed. "This gentleman is my son's teacher, not his father, but if he doesn't mind, I have no objection to a tour. If you're sure it's safe."

"Oh, yes, ma'am. I'd never put a passenger in the way of danger."

Charles nodded and thanked the conductor. "How about if we do that on our return trip? Perhaps when we reach Magnolia Junction?" He signed to Jeremiah as he spoke to the conductor.

"All right. That's fine, I guess," Jeremiah signed back.

The matter settled, Charles leaned back and closed his eyes. He was pretty sure Jeremiah would change his mind about working on the railroad once he paid a visit to the coal car. But it couldn't hurt the young man to experience another slice of life.

When they arrived in Atlanta, Jeremiah tried to act nonchalant, but his eyes widened at the teeming crowds. They barely had time to hire a cab and ride to the court-house where Trent's and Mrs. Saunders's attorneys met them. Charles nodded in satisfaction to see that Jeremiah and his mother were well represented.

The trial seemed almost anticlimactic after the emotional hearing they'd had at the sheriff's office in Rome.

In spite of two bogus witnesses, who tried to assert that Frank Saunders had abused his son, the boy's own horrified denial as well as his mother's convinced the jury. Under questioning from Mrs. Saunders's attorney, one of the "witnesses" admitted under oath that he'd been paid to lie on the stand.

In less than two hours, Edward Saunders had been convicted of fraud and child beating.

Satisfaction ran through Charles as he walked outside with Trent, Mrs. Saunders and Jeremiah.

The attorneys had assured them that one of the stipulations of any future parole for Saunders would be that he go nowhere near his sister-in-law, his nephew or their property.

After a lingering and luxurious midday meal at the hotel, Mrs. Saunders expressed a need to go shopping, so Trent volunteered to accompany her.

Charles took Jeremiah to several museums, saving his favorite for last. He knew from Helen that Jeremiah was fascinated with the Battle of Atlanta, and had perused the history book containing the story over and over.

"Let's go in this building, Jeremiah. They have a painting I think you'll be interested in."

Jeremiah groaned, but followed his mentor up the steps and through the massive door.

They stepped into the reception area and Charles asked to see the Cyclorama. Jeremiah gave him a curious glance, but the receptionist smiled and directed them toward a large room at the side.

A tour was beginning as they walked in and the narrator motioned for them to take a seat with the others.

Jeremiah drew in a breath when he saw the panorama stretching out on all sides. As the narrator gave details of the Battle of Atlanta, the painting seemed to take on a life of its own.

By the time Charles and his student left, Jeremiah was almost ashen.

"Let's go get something to drink," Charles said. "How does hot cocoa sound?"

Jeremiah nodded, but didn't speak until he sat on a chair across the small table from Charles. "It was like being there."

Charles nodded. "A company called Panorama is responsible for the Cyclorama of the Battle of Atlanta. And I agree. It's almost like being there."

"But, it shows the Yankees' victory more than anything."

"Yes, believe it or not, the painting first traveled with a circus, but when the circus got to Atlanta, the people here were furious and refused to look at it. The circus eventually went bankrupt. In fact, the animals are mostly in the zoo here. Would you like to see them before we return to the hotel?"

"No, sir. I'd rather not."

"One day I'd like for you to look at the painting again. There is much more than the victory of the Northern troops depicted there."

"I know." Jeremiah nodded. "I saw a lot more, really. It was horrible, wasn't it?"

"Yes. It certainly was. For both sides."

They finished their hot drinks and headed back to the hotel, where they found an excited Trent.

"Where's Ma?"

"Upstairs packing all the new clothes she just bought. She said to tell you to come up, if you like."

Jeremiah headed for the elevator and soon was out of sight.

Trent gripped Charles's arm. "I just got some news that might relate to Lily Ann."

Charles gave his friend a wary look. Lily Ann's accident had happened at Trent's house, when a runaway horse had kicked the little girl and she'd fallen, hitting her head. Or had the horse kicked her in the head? Well, regardless, the poor child had ended up totally blind. Since the parents refused to send her away to school, she became the only blind student at Quincy, boarding through the week and going home on weekends. When Charles first arrived at Quincy, Trent seemed obsessed with finding a cure for the child, but lately, he'd seemed to have given up hope.

Charles followed Trent into the dining room, where they ordered coffee. "So tell me about it."

"There's a new hospital here in Atlanta called Grady Hospital. They have a trauma department doing all sorts of research. I spoke to one of the specialists about Lily Ann. Told him all the details and all the doctors I'd spoken to."

"He offered hope?"

"Well, it depends. He agreed that there is probably nothing at this point that medicine or surgery can do. Although, of course, he'd need to examine her to say conclusively. Which, of course, her parents won't allow anymore."

"Then what has you so excited?"

"According to this doctor and his colleagues, blindness that has occurred from trauma has been known to reverse itself by another traumatic incident."

Charles stared. "I don't understand. That would require another accident."

Trent pressed his lips together. "Or a carefully orchestrated one."

"You mean you'd make something happen to Lily Ann?"

"No, of course not. It would have to be done under a specialist's supervision."

Charles frowned. "I don't know, Trent. Are you sure you're not grasping at straws again?"

Once more, Trent's lips tightened. "Lily Ann has to see again."

Charles looked at his friend and sighed. If he didn't know Trent better, he'd think the man was going mad. As it was, he realized that his friend was excited because his hope for the child's vision had been restored.

"I'll be praying about it, Trent."

"That's all I ask."

Two hours later they boarded the train and headed home. Excitement ran through Charles as thoughts of Livvy bombarded his mind. He could hardly wait to see her again.

As Charles had expected, it only took a visit to the coal car for Jeremiah to lose interest in railroading.

Jeremiah came out into the fresh air at Magnolia Junction with his nose turned up. "It stinks in there! I think I'd better stay with farming."

Charles grinned. Of course, everyone loved the smell of horse manure.

"Livvy, the divinity is about to boil over." Ma's panicked cry brought Livvy back from the dream world she'd been living in lately. She rushed to stir the candy down.

"Sorry, Ma. It's safe." But Livvy's voice shook. What a mess she would have had to clean up if the stuff really had boiled over.

It would take two of them to get it poured out in just the right time. Livvy couldn't see what the big deal about divinity was, anyway. She thought the stuff tasted downright nasty and much preferred fudge of almost any flavor. But the older ladies all swore by their divinity. Probably because it was so difficult to make.

An hour later, several batches of divinity stood in small mounds and Livvy sang as she stirred peanut butter fudge.

"I'm glad to see you're in a happier mood than you were earlier, daughter." Mama smiled as she melted butter for the fudge.

"I am happy, Mama." Livvy's lips curled upward, testifying to the truth of her words.

"Looking forward to the festival and dance tomorrow night, dear?"

"Yes, ma'am. It should be a lot of fun, don't you think so?"

"Be careful if you take part in the three-legged race. Remember the year you fell and skinned your knee so badly?"

Livvy laughed. "Mama! I think I'm a mite old for those sorts of games, don't you?"

"Only if you think you are." Mama's eyes twinkled.

"Yes, ma'am. I certainly do think I am."

"What are you looking forward to the most? The dance, maybe?" Once again, the twinkle.

Livvy sighed. She should have known. Mama was teasing.

"Is Charles picking you up, dear?"

"No, he has to ride over with the wagons from the school. He and Felicity and Howard and Hannah Wilson have to chaperone, you know."

"Not the whole evening, I hope." Ma pulled a wooden spoon from the candy mixture and allowed a small amount to drop in a cup of cold water.

"Well, no. They'll have more volunteers once they get to the Bineses'. Everyone sort of takes turns so the teachers can have some fun, too." Livvy looked at the sample in the cup. "It's not ready yet, Mama."

Mama sighed and laid the spoon on her chicken-shaped

spoon rest. "I know. I always get in a hurry when we're making fudge."

By midafternoon the candy they'd promised was all done and boxed up.

"What do you think, Livvy? Shall we go ahead and take these over to the Bineses' so we won't have to load them up tomorrow night?"

"Hmm. That's fine with me, Mama. It'll be nice to simply concentrate on getting ready tomorrow and driving over."

"I agree." Mama walked to the back porch and came back with several baskets. When they had everything packed up, Mama asked Hank to hitch up the buggy for them.

The day was sunny and mild as Livvy took the reins and drove from the churchyard. "Oh, I hope the weather stays nice until after the festival."

"Yes. Me, too. Remember the year we had an early snow and had to cancel it?"

"Yes, we must have had five inches that year."

"The most I've seen in this part of Georgia. Of course, five inches wouldn't have seemed like much back in Maine, where I grew up."

"Do you ever miss it, Mama?"

"Maine? I did at first. But now I can't imagine living anywhere but Georgia." She patted Livvy on the leg and smiled. "Of course, being with your father helped me adjust to a new location mighty fast."

"I can't imagine leaving Georgia and moving far away from you and Pa." Livvy glanced at her ma, wondering. She barely remembered the two visits from her grandparents before they both passed away years ago.

"When you fall in love, you'll go anywhere as long as you can be with him."

Livvy had always known that her parents loved each other, but she'd never given it much thought.

What if Charles did propose? He was a teacher. What if another teaching position should come up that he wanted to pursue? Would she be willing to go with him?

She needed to think this over carefully. Up to now, she'd only thought of her feelings for him. But there was much more than feelings involved in a relationship. What if she had to choose between Charles and her parents?

Scoffing inwardly at herself, she smiled at her mother and pulled into the Bineses' barnyard. As Pa often said, she was counting her chickens before they were hatched. Charles had yet to propose.

Livvy was surprised to see several neighbors there. They must have had the same idea she and Mama had. Fresh-baked goods lined the tables. And Ezra Bines had set his iron barbecue pot over a section of the pit. He always did a variety of barbecue types. Pork, beef and even mutton sometimes.

Part of the barn floor had been cleared for the dance, and the sides and corners of the room were lined with booths for the fund-raiser. Excitement ran through Livvy. It was going to be a great festival.

Even Mama seemed excited as they drove home. When they pulled into the barn, Hank was waiting, so Livvy thanked him and went to the house with Mama.

The chicken stew was simmering on the back of the stove.

"Livvy, would you stir the dumplings in, please? I'll pour the drinks and set the table. Your pa should be in soon. He's been finishing up his sermon for Sunday morning."

By the time supper was ready, Pa stepped into the hall from his study.

"Pa, perfect timing."

Pa rubbed his hands together and smiled. "I smelled the chicken and dumplings. Let me go wash up. Be right back."

Within a few minutes the three of them sat around the table.

Pa bowed his head and Livvy and her mother followed suit.

"Heavenly Father, we thank You for being with us today and every day. Thank You for our wonderful family. I pray, Lord, You will help us as we go through the rest of this day. Help us with any decisions we need to make. And help us to always be kind to each other. We thank You for this wonderful food, supplied from Your bounty. In Jesus's name. Amen."

Livvy stared at her Pa for a moment, wondering if he'd read her mind. Of course not. This sort of thing happened often in their home. God must have whispered a word in Pa's ear. The Lord knew she needed wisdom about possible decisions.

She glanced around at the cozy family time. Her parents were laughing over something Pa had said. *Oh, Lord. Could I leave them if Charles asked me to?* A quiet knowing flowed through her. Oh, yes. She would go with Charles to the ends of the earth. That is, if he asked her.

Chapter 19

The tantalizing scent of spiced apple cider drifted through the strong smell of wood smoke and barbecue as Livvy stepped into the Bineses' barn with Mama and Pa.

"Umm. It smells so good in here." She gave a sniff of appreciation, then another.

"Yes, it does. I love the smells of fall." Ma looked so pretty tonight and Pa was holding her hand.

"Yes. And winter." Although the difference was minuscule.

A squawk and whine came from the stage where the musicians were tuning their instruments. Livvy clapped her hands over her ears.

Eddy Bines stood in front of the enormous iron stove at the rear of the barn, cramming logs in.

Mama frowned. "Oh, dear. I hope Eddy doesn't overdo it."

"Me, too. Once the dancing starts, the room will heat up fast."

Livvy glanced around. The children and staff from

Quincy School hadn't yet arrived. A little quiver of anticipation wiggled through her chest at the thought of Charles. Would this be the night?

"Livvy! You're here." Carrie Ann sashayed up and grabbed Livvy's hand. "Someone wants to talk to you."

At Mrs. Shepherd's raised eyebrows, Carrie Ann blushed. "I'm sorry, Mrs. Shepherd, Reverend Shepherd. How are you tonight?"

Livvy grinned as Mama gave the girl a tight smile. Mama never could abide rudeness. Especially from young people.

"I'm doing very well, Carrie Ann." Mrs. Shepherd's half smile spoke volumes.

Carrie Ann cleared her throat. "I think Mama and Mrs. Couch are over by the jelly booth if you'd like to talk to them."

"Thank you. Perhaps later. I believe my husband wishes me to stay with him for the moment. But you girls go ahead."

Carrie Ann pulled Livvy aside. "Now, Livvy, I know you have your cap set on Charles. Everyone knows except him, the dunce."

"Carrie Ann. That's not nice."

The girl shrugged and Livvy shook her head. "If you're matchmaking again, stop it."

"Well, really, you shouldn't put all your eggs in one basket, as they say. Especially when someone else is mooning over you. She gave a knowing look and nodded toward the side wall.

Livvy, irritated, glanced in that direction. Rudy Baker was walking toward them, a hopeful look on his face. Now what? She couldn't be rude to him.

"What have you done, Carrie Ann?" she asked through clamped teeth.

Innocence shone all over Carrie's face. "Nothing. I just told him you were here and if he would like a dance later, he'd better not wait to ask."

"Well, if that's all. But I wish you'd stop doing this sort of thing. I've known Rudy since he was born. There's not a thing wrong with him, but I'm not interested."

"Oh, Livvy. I think he's right handsome."

"Then why don't *you* go after him?"

Horror crossed Carrie Ann's pretty face. "Eww. He's way too old for me."

"He's two years younger than I am. That's not too old for you."

"Well, but he wants to get married and I'm nowhere near ready for that. Besides, he only has eyes for you. Shh. He's almost here."

Rudy approached, a grin on his handsome face. "Hi, Livvy."

"Hi, Rudy. Haven't seen you in a while. How are your folks?"

"They're doing great. The store's keeping them busy most days. They stayed home tonight. Said they didn't want to ride all the way over and back from Magnolia Junction."

Livvy nodded. "Well, you be sure to tell them I said hello."

"All right, I will." He bit his lip and cleared his throat. "Uh… Livvy, I was wondering if I could have a dance later."

"I'm sure you can, Rudy. During the square dance, all right?"

A momentary disappointment crossed his face, but he smiled. "Thanks. I'll be looking forward to it. Would you like some punch?"

"No, but I'd love some hot spiced cider."

"Oh, that sounds good to me, too. I'll get us both a cup

and be right back." He glanced at Carrie. "How about you, Carrie?"

"No, thanks. I'm going to talk to Saundra."

As soon as Rudy was out of sight, Livvy grabbed Carrie Ann's sleeve. "Don't you dare leave my side as long as Rudy is here with me. Do you understand?"

"Oh, all right. Don't be so snippety." Carrie giggled. "The man is crazy about you."

"I only hope I'm not encouraging him. It's hard to draw the line between that and politeness. And I will never be interested in Rudy as anything more than a friend."

"Even if Charles doesn't propose?"

"Even then."

Carrie Ann gave her a look of disbelief. "I don't understand you at all, Olivia Shepherd. Don't you want a home of your own and children? Chances are you'd eventually fall in love with whoever you married."

Livvy closed her eyes momentarily. "Carrie Ann, no more on the subject, please."

"Oh, all right. Here comes Rudy with the drinks."

Livvy opened her eyes in time to see Carrie slip away. She would give her a piece of her mind later. She forced a smile as Rudy handed her a steaming cup. Fragrant spices drifted up and she inhaled in appreciation. "Thanks, Rudy. Just what I wanted."

A commotion at the door drew their attention. Livvy brightened. "Oh, it's Quincy School. Let's go greet them." She headed toward Felicity. Patrick and Helen were with them. They must have been helping out.

Livvy was immediately surrounded by "her girls" before she had a chance to speak to Helen. She glanced at Rudy, who looked a little intimidated. He grinned at her. "I'll see you for that dance, then."

Livvy perused the boys as they came in, shoving and laughing. But where was Charles?

She turned back to the girls. "Where's Mr. Charles?"

Lily Ann, who was boarding at the school this weekend while her parents were out of town, piped up. "He and Miss Wilson had to go to Magnolia Junction. They'll be here later."

Shock ran through Livvy. Charles and Hannah Wilson? She had never pictured or even imagined those two together. Nausea rose up in her stomach and she fought back tears. *Stop it, Olivia. Just stop it. You've always known that Charles only wanted friendship from you.* But Hannah Wilson? She'd never seen any indication of interest. But what did she know about men anyway? Maybe their interest didn't always show.

"Are you all right, Miss Livvy?" Margaret, with a rare note of concern for someone else, frowned and pulled at Livvy's sleeve.

Olivia smiled and took a deep breath. "Yes. I must have had a moment of getting overheated. But I'll be fine now."

Helen strolled by on her husband's arm and stopped. "Did the girls tell you where Charles and Hannah are?"

"Yes, they did," Livvy murmured.

"Good. He specifically told us to let you know."

Well. The very idea. Now he was rubbing it in. She sighed as Helen walked away. That thought wasn't fair. Charles had always shared everything with Livvy. How was he to know it would hit her heart like salt on a wound?

How could she have been so wrong? All the signs from Charles she'd thought she was reading had been nothing but her hopeful imagination. Like a schoolgirl. She mustn't let him know. He'd hurt for her and she would be humiliated. She had to let him think she was all right with it. But how?

She turned and saw Rudy talking with a group of young men. Rudy. She hated to get his hopes up and then dash them. Maybe she wouldn't dash them. Perhaps Carrie Ann was right. After all, every woman wanted a home and family. And maybe she could learn to love Rudy. Then Charles and his precious Hannah would never know they'd crushed her tonight.

Trembling, she stepped toward Rudy.

Charles couldn't help but grin as he half glanced toward the excited young woman who stood beside him on the depot platform. She'd said that she and Dr. Monroe were good friends, but he was beginning to wonder if they might be more. Or at least on Hannah's part. Her pretty brown eyes sparkled and the tip of her tongue darted out to moisten pink lips. Most of all, her cheeks were rosy, and not merely from the chill in the air, if he knew anything about girls.

He grinned. After all, it was rosy cheeks that had first indicated to him that he might have a chance with Livvy. That perhaps she saw him as more than the best friend she'd spent time with for the past six years. He pulled out his pocket watch and looked at it again for the sixth or seventh time. The consarned train was late. He'd thought to have his charges back to the festival by now and be drinking a cup of cider with Livvy. Then later, after the square dancing, the closing waltz.

Patrick and Helen had agreed to ride back to the school with the children and other volunteers so Charles could take Livvy home in the school's buggy. After all, her parents would need theirs and four was too much company for what he had in mind.

He reached into his pocket once more and this time his hand cupped a small box. Tempted to draw it out and gaze at the ring again, he resisted the temptation and turned to Hannah. He caught her in the act of craning her neck to look down the track. Just as a kid would do. He held back the laugh that threatened to surface and just then a whistle blew from down the track.

Within a few minutes the train rounded the bend and by the time the tall, broad-shouldered doctor stepped down, Hannah stood straight, prim and proper.

Charles's suspicions were confirmed when the man's eyes lit up the moment his gaze rested on Hannah.

Stepping forward, Charles introduced himself and shook hands.

"Oh, yes, Waverly. Dr. Quincy has told me a lot about you."

"Yes, he's spoken a lot about you, as well. He's very impressed with your work at the school in Kansas City. But basically you're here to observe Lily Ann, I understand."

They retrieved the man's luggage from the baggage car and Charles led the way to the buggy, where he deposited the luggage in the backseat.

On the way back to the Bineses' barn, Dr. Monroe and Hannah laughed and talked about incidents they'd shared and friends they had in common while Hannah had attended classes at the school where he spent his senior year.

"Remember the toboggan race?" Giggles pealed from Hannah's throat.

"Do I?" A booming laugh followed the giggles. "If you want to call it that. Half the toboggans and sleds never made it off the top of the hill."

"That's because Frank Calvin sabotaged all the runners."

"Really? I hadn't heard that. But I left for Grady Hospital about that time."

"Yes, I know. You forgot to say goodbye." Hannah's voice grew quiet.

"Actually, I didn't forget. It was such a sudden move. They offered me the position, which came with free training. I did tell your friend, Bonnie, to tell you, though, and gave her an address where you could write."

"You did? Bonnie came down with pneumonia about that time. By the time she was over it, she was quite weak and her parents took her home."

"I'm sorry, Hannah. I didn't know. When I didn't hear from you, I assumed you didn't care to correspond."

Charles listened with interest. Amazing how people's relationships could fall victim to misunderstandings. Well, there was one misunderstanding he'd clear up tonight. He'd tell Olivia he loved her and ask her to spend the rest of her life with him.

Charles heard the music before he saw the barn and he straightened his back in anticipation.

He guided the horses into the drive and reined in at the makeshift hitching post.

Dr. Monroe jumped down and helped Hannah out of the buggy.

"We'll need to transfer your luggage to one of the wagons." Charles smiled. "I'll be using the buggy for something else after the festivities tonight."

The doctor nodded. "Show me where to put the suitcases and I'll take care of that. I'll be right in."

Charles took Hannah's elbow and led her toward the festively decorated barn. Two lines—one of ladies and one of gents—faced each other.

Charles scanned the lines and spotted Livvy across from Rudy Baker, who gazed at her with soulful eyes. Poor Rudy. He could just get over it and find another girl.

The dance started and they crossed over and joined hands, dancing down the aisle until they reached the end.

Livvy lifted her eyes and her gaze met his then wandered over to Hannah who still stood beside him. A frozen expression crossed her face, then she glanced up at Rudy and threw him a coquettish smile. Rudy looked like he'd pass out, then he grabbed her hands and do-si-do'd away.

Charles stared at Livvy. Why had she ignored him? Surely she didn't think he and Hannah… But Helen was supposed to tell her what was going on. He needed to find Helen…now.

At that moment, the door opened with a gust of wind and the doctor entered. Depositing Hannah on the doctor's arm, he went in search of Helen.

Chapter 20

Oh, dear, what had she done? Sure she was upset about Charles and Hannah, but was that any reason to lead Rudy on the way she had? Why, she'd been downright flirting with him all evening. He was sure to expect to dance the last waltz with her. Then maybe he'd ask to take her home.

He'd gone to get her a slice of pecan pie. She plopped down at a table that was mercifully empty of people. How was she going to get out of this predicament? And without hurting Rudy too much?

"Livvy, I need to talk to you." Helen swooped down on her and sat beside her.

"All right, Helen. What do you need to talk about?"

"I need to know what the girls told you about Charles and Hannah."

Livvy pressed her lips together. "Just that they had gone to Magnolia Junction together and would be here later. And there they are."

"Where exactly are they, Livvy?"

"I don't know. Should I have kept them in my sight?" She glanced around. "Over there. See?"

"I see Hannah, but that isn't Charles with her." Helen raised her eyebrows. "Look again."

Livvy gazed at Hannah. The man at her elbow, peering into her soft brown eyes, was a stranger.

"Who in the world is that?"

"His name is Daniel Monroe. A specialist from Grady Hospital. Dr. Monroe has come here at Dr. Quincy's request to observe Lily Ann."

Livvy frowned. "I don't understand. What does that have to do with Charles and Hannah?"

"Nothing, except that Charles went to Magnolia Junction to meet the doctor's train and bring him back to the festival. Hannah went along because she and Dr. Monroe are longtime friends."

"But, I thought…"

"I know what you thought and so does Charles. He's devastated."

"He is?" Charles was upset because she'd misunderstood?

"Of course, silly. Charles is very much in love with you." Helen shook her head and looked like she'd love to shake Livvy, as well. "And, for your information, he told Patrick and Trent that very thing."

A burst of joy swelled in Livvy's heart. "Where is he?"

"The last time I saw him he was heading out the front door. I don't know if he left or went outside."

Livvy gasped. She'd put on a terrible display with Rudy just to try to make Charles think she was interested in the handsome young man. Now it had backfired on her, plus sent the wrong message to Rudy.

What should she do? She certainly couldn't just drop

Rudy like a hot potato. She must find a way to let him down easily. But what about the waltz? He'd expect it now.

Her hands shook as she saw Rudy coming toward her, pie in hand. She groaned. "I've led Rudy on shamefully."

Helen tried to hide a grin. "You panicked. He'll get over it."

Livvy tossed her an uncertain glance. "Are you sure?"

"Yes, and the sooner you let him know, the better," she cautioned. "Otherwise, it gets harder to do. Once he knows you mean it, I'll warrant you, he'll start looking over the other girls."

"That doesn't sound much like devotion to me." After all, Rudy had been after her for years.

"Believe me. He's only devoted because he thinks there is still a chance. How old is he? Twenty-three or twenty-four?"

"Yes, nearly twenty-four." Come to think of it, hadn't Livvy suggested to Carrie Ann earlier that she should go after Rudy?

"Here you go, Livvy." Rudy set the pie on the table in front of her. And she noticed that he'd dropped the "Miss" when he spoke to her. Oh, this was worse than she'd thought.

"Howdy, Mrs. Flannigan."

"Hello, Rudy."

He turned back to Livvy. "You don't mind if I call you Livvy, do you?"

All right. She needed to handle it right here. "Of course not, Rudy. Goodness, we've been friends for years. You didn't call me 'Miss' when we were in school, did you?"

Disappointment flooded his face. He was getting the point.

"No." He gave a shaky laugh. "But we were children then."

"Oh, well, what's a given name between lifelong friends?" She smiled. A different type of smile from the ones she'd tossed his way since Charles and Hannah had arrived. Maybe Rudy would think he'd imagined the others. Then she wouldn't need to say anything about her actions.

She was happy Mama and Pa had gone home before she'd started her shenanigans. She wouldn't have been able to hide anything from Mama.

"I really enjoyed the square dances, Rudy. Thanks for being my partner tonight."

He nodded. "It was my pleasure, Miss Olivia." His lips curved in a sad smile. "And now, I'd best be getting home. We're trying a new church in Magnolia Junction in the morning. Mother is very excited about it."

As he turned to go, Livvy knew she couldn't let him leave this way. It wasn't honest. It wasn't right.

"Wait, Rudy. Will you sit down for a minute? I need to tell you something."

He turned and took a seat at the table, across from her.

Helen jumped up. "Well, I need to find my husband. It's almost time for the waltz."

She was gone in an instant.

Livvy raised her eyes to Rudy's waiting, questioning gaze.

"I'm so sorry, Rudy." She swallowed and fought back tears. "You see, I'm in love with Charles Waverly. I was hurt because I thought he cared for someone else. Not wanting him to know, I'm ashamed to say I used you, Rudy. I flirted and led you on to try to prove a point. And you didn't deserve that. You've never been anything but kind to me."

His face turned ashen for a moment, then he nodded and stood. "As I said, I'll be leaving now." Without another word he stalked over to the coatrack and got his overcoat and hat.

Livvy watched in misery as he shoved open the barn door and stepped through.

Charles watched with interest as Rudy Baker slammed out of the barn, mounted his horse and took off down the road like fury was after him.

Hope rose. Maybe things weren't that bad after all. He heard strains of an unfamiliar waltz tune drifting from the barn. He'd better get in there, lickety-split.

He charged through the doors and breathed a sigh of relief. The Monroe Brothers were tuning up while folks finished up their refreshments and began to pair up.

Charles glanced around and paused as his eyes met Livvy's deep blue ones. She caught her breath and continued to walk toward him. He met her and took her hands.

"Livvy."

"Charles. I'm so sorry. I misunderstood. I should have asked Helen instead of jumping to conclusions."

"It doesn't matter. You know now, that's enough." He tightened his hands as hers trembled.

The fiddle and accordion picked up the beat. "Okay, folks. It's almost time to go home. Let's close the evening with this beautiful waltz, written by a friend of mine down Missouri way. You may have heard it, but probably not, seeing as it's not yet published. But you will before long, I'm sure. It's called the 'Missouri Waltz.'"

Charles turned to Livvy and found her waiting with a shy smile. "May I have this dance, Miss Olivia Shepherd?"

"Yes, you certainly may, Mr. Charles Waverly."

They walked to the dance floor and their hands met in midair. Charles's other hand found its home at Livvy's waist and they swung into the waltz. His heart thumped wildly and his head felt like a million wings pounded inside. *Dear God, how can I ever thank You for Livvy's love? I know she loves me, even though we haven't yet spoken of it. Thank You. Thank You.*

He gazed down at her upturned face. Her eyes were closed and a tiny smile tilted her lips.

All too soon, Silas Monroe's fiddle sang the final notes of the lovely "Missouri Waltz." Charles didn't know if the song would grow in popularity or not, but he'd never forget it as long as he lived.

Livvy opened her eyes at the closing notes of the song and looked full into Charles's beautiful brown eyes. He did love her. She could see the love shining from his eyes. How could she ever have doubted? No more hiding her feelings from him. She smiled and put all her love for him in that smile.

She didn't even turn at the giggles behind them. Molly and Lily Ann. She felt a tug at her elbow and sighed as she turned to gaze down at the girls. At the excitement in their eyes, she smiled.

"Miss Livvy," Molly stage-whispered. "Are you and Mr. Charles in love?"

At that, Livvy's face flamed. "Molly, that was rude. You mustn't ask personal questions."

The girl grinned. "Sorry." And in a torrent of giggles, the two girls ran across the dance floor to Felicity.

"Shall we get out of here?" Charles took her elbow and began to guide her toward the door.

"But don't you have to help get the children home?"

Charles grinned down at her. "Not this time. Patrick and Helen are filling in for me and I'm keeping the buggy to take you home. That is, if the idea is agreeable to you."

"It certainly is." A ripple of excitement tickled her stomach.

They slipped away unnoticed and soon were tucked cozily beneath a warm lap blanket in the buggy. Livvy drew her coat up tightly around her throat and tucked her scarf in.

Charles took one of her mittened hands in his. "Warm enough, sweetheart?"

"I am now." That "sweetheart" would warm her all the way home.

"I'd planned to ask if we could stop somewhere to talk, but it's too cold for you out here. Do you think your parents would mind if we spent a little while in the parlor?"

"They won't mind at all. Pa has often said he'd rather I be at home where he knows I'm safe."

"I'm sure I'd feel the same if I had a daughter," Charles said. "So let's head for the parsonage."

They laughed at every word they said on the way home, and pulled into the parsonage yard still laughing. Livvy's eyes sparkled as she waited for Charles to tie the buggy to the hitching post.

He took her hand and they stepped into the kitchen, still warm and fragrant with scents of cookies and pies.

Pa was waiting in the parlor, as Livvy knew he'd be. He rose, yawning. "Hello, daughter, Charles. Did you enjoy the festival?"

"Oh, yes, Pa."

"More than I can say, sir."

Livvy's father turned knowing eyes on them both and gave a nod and a smile. "Well, you two don't need me. I think I'll turn in."

They said their good-nights, then Livvy and Charles turned to each other. For a moment neither said anything. They simply gazed into each other's eyes.

"My sweet Olivia, before I utter another word, I have to say this. I love you, with all my heart. I guess because of our deep, long-standing friendship, it took me a while to realize my true feelings. But there's no doubt in my mind. I love you, my darling, totally and forever."

Livvy's heart sang. Yes, it was time. This was the magical, wonderful night. "And I love you, too, my precious Charles. I've loved you since the first time I set eyes on your darling face. And, never fear, I was twenty."

A laugh escaped his lips for a moment, then he took her into his arms. "And you'll marry me, won't you?"

"Of course. That is, if you ask me."

Instantly, he fell to his knees and pulled out a small box. "Livvy, will you make me the happiest man in the world and spend your life with me?"

"With all my heart, I will."

He slipped the ring onto her finger and stood, taking her into his arms again. She raised her lips and met his kiss. As his lips pressed against hers, she knew the most amazing thing in the world was happening.

Epilogue

Mama shooed Carrie Ann and little Bridget Bines out of Livvy's bedroom. There was a time for bridesmaids and flower girls and a time for mother and daughter.

"You're the most beautiful bride I've ever seen, my Livvy." Mama adjusted the veil again and blinked back the tears that threatened to escape. "But I refuse to cry while you walk down the aisle."

Livvy smiled. "I don't mind if you do, Mama. I know you're happy for Charles and me. And I'll miss you, too."

"I hope you didn't mind the little talk we had last night. I know you're not eighteen, but still."

"I didn't mind, Mama." Livvy blushed. "To be honest, I'm very grateful. The truth is lovely. The fabrications and half truths I've heard since I was fourteen were pretty scary sometimes." Although how she'd not known more at her age was a mystery. Maybe because she hadn't wanted to know? Thank the Lord for a mama who loved her enough to have a face-to-face talk about the wedding night.

Livvy glanced out the window at the live oak right outside. She was glad for the splash of green among the lovely myriad autumn colors, although she was still happy they'd decided on a fall wedding. Well, to be fair, she'd decided. Charles would have married her the day after he'd proposed.

Her stomach did a flip-flop. Her wedding day. After all those years of yearning and to finally know Charles had loved her all the time. But she didn't regret that they'd had the seven years to get to know each other better. And to become good friends.

And now. Something wonderful was coming to their relationship. Much better than friendship, although that would always remain.

A tap on the door warned her that it was time to go. She glanced around the room she'd dreamed and cried and laughed in for as long as she could remember.

Mama opened the door and Carrie Ann stuck her head in, her eyes dancing. "The buggy is outside."

Livvy met her mother's eyes and smiled. Bridget and Carrie got into the buggy and then Mama, followed by Livvy in order to make sure her dress didn't become crushed.

Five minutes later, they stopped at the church steps. *Lord, is this really happening? I feel as if I might wake up any moment and find I've been dreaming again.*

As they stepped through the door, Jeremiah held his arm out for Mama and they walked down the aisle to her seat.

Strains of the classical piece Livvy had chosen and now couldn't remember drifted down the aisle. Let's see. Mendelssohn, but that was for later. What was that piece?

Carrie Ann patted her and started down the aisle. Livvy swallowed as Bridget started a little early but then did a beautiful job with the flower petals.

The music changed to the "Bridal Chorus," and suddenly Pa was by her side. A preacher friend from Magnolia Junction stood behind the pulpit for now.

A sea of faces blurred before her as she stepped down the aisle on Pa's arm. She blinked and all was clear again. Charles stood waiting for her. Did he have tears in his eyes? Or was that her own tears she saw?

The next thing she knew, Pa was placing her hand in Charles's. The warmth of her bridegroom's hand sent a matching warmth up her wrist and into her arm. She took a deep breath and smiled up into his warm, brown, adoring eyes.

Pa went to stand behind the pulpit. "Dearly Beloved. We have come today to join this man and this woman in holy matrimony." Pa's voice cracked. He gave Livvy an apologetic smile, then continued.

Livvy tried to concentrate on Pa's words, but all she could see or hear was Charles. Then she did hear as her father said, "I now pronounce you man and wife. You may kiss the bride."

If Livvy had thought the few kisses they'd allowed themselves this past year were thrilling, they paled beside the first one she received as Charles's bride.

As his lips pressed against hers, the kiss was tender and loving but so much more. It promised many more to come. Livvy smiled and flung her arms around Charles, kissing him back with joyful abandon.

"I love you, my precious Livvy," he whispered so she alone could hear.

"And I love you, my darling husband."

"I suppose we have to greet everyone before we go." Charles's eyes sparkled.

"I'm afraid so, dear." Livvy grinned and they turned and walked down the aisle as husband and wife.

* * * * *

REQUEST YOUR FREE BOOKS!

2 FREE CHRISTIAN NOVELS
PLUS 2
FREE
MYSTERY GIFTS

HEARTSONG
PRESENTS

YES! Please send me 2 Free Heartsong Presents novels and my 2 FREE mystery gifts (gifts are worth about $10). After receiving them, if I don't wish to receive any more books I can return the shipping statement marked "cancel." If I don't cancel, I will receive 4 brand-new novels every month and be billed just $4.24 per book in the U.S. and $5.24 per book in Canada. That's a savings of at least 20% off the cover price. It's quite a bargain! Shipping and handling is just 50¢ per book in the U.S. and 75¢ per book in Canada.* I understand that accepting the 2 free books and gifts places me under no obligation to buy anything. I can always return a shipment and cancel at any time. Even if I never buy another book, the two free books and gifts are mine to keep forever.

159/359 HDN FVYK

Name	(PLEASE PRINT)

Address	Apt. #

City	State	Zip

Signature (if under 18, a parent or guardian must sign)

Mail to the Harlequin® Reader Service:
IN U.S.A.: P.O. Box 1867, Buffalo, NY 14240-1867

* Terms and prices subject to change without notice. Prices do not include applicable taxes. Sales tax applicable in N.Y. This offer is limited to one order per household. Not valid for current subscribers to Heartsong Presents books. All orders subject to credit approval. Credit or debit balances in a customer's account(s) may be offset by any other outstanding balance owed by or to the customer. Please allow 4 to 6 weeks for delivery. Offer available while quantities last. Offer valid only in the U.S.

Your Privacy—The Harlequin® Reader Service is committed to protecting your privacy. Our Privacy Policy is available online at www.ReaderService.com or upon request from the Harlequin Reader Service.
We make a portion of our mailing list available to reputable third parties that offer products we believe may interest you. If you prefer that we not exchange your name with third parties, or if you wish to clarify or modify your communication preferences, please visit us at www.ReaderService.com/consumerschoice or write to us at Harlequin Reader Service Preference Service, P.O. Box 9062, Buffalo, NY 14269. Include your complete name and address.

HSPDIR13R

REQUEST YOUR FREE BOOKS!

2 FREE INSPIRATIONAL NOVELS
PLUS 2
FREE
MYSTERY GIFTS

Love Inspired

YES! Please send me 2 FREE Love Inspired® novels and my 2 FREE mystery gifts (gifts are worth about $10). After receiving them, if I don't wish to receive any more books, I can return the shipping statement marked "cancel." If I don't cancel, I will receive 6 brand-new novels every month and be billed just $4.74 per book in the U.S. or $5.24 per book in Canada. That's a savings of at least 21% off the cover price. It's quite a bargain! Shipping and handling is just 50¢ per book in the U.S. and 75¢ per book in Canada.* I understand that accepting the 2 free books and gifts places me under no obligation to buy anything. I can always return a shipment and cancel at any time. Even if I never buy another book, the two free books and gifts are mine to keep forever.

105/305 IDN F49N

Name _____ (PLEASE PRINT) _____

Address _____ Apt. # _____

City _____ State/Prov. _____ Zip/Postal Code _____

Signature (if under 18, a parent or guardian must sign)

Mail to the **Harlequin® Reader Service:**
IN U.S.A.: P.O. Box 1867, Buffalo, NY 14240-1867
IN CANADA: P.O. Box 609, Fort Erie, Ontario L2A 5X3

**Are you a subscriber to Love Inspired books
and want to receive the larger-print edition?
Call 1-800-873-8635 or visit www.ReaderService.com.**

* Terms and prices subject to change without notice. Prices do not include applicable taxes. Sales tax applicable in N.Y. Canadian residents will be charged applicable taxes. Offer not valid in Quebec. This offer is limited to one order per household. Not valid for current subscribers to Love Inspired books. All orders subject to credit approval. Credit or debit balances in a customer's account(s) may be offset by any other outstanding balance owed by or to the customer. Please allow 4 to 6 weeks for delivery. Offer available while quantities last.

Your Privacy—The Harlequin® Reader Service is committed to protecting your privacy. Our Privacy Policy is available online at www.ReaderService.com or upon request from the Harlequin Reader Service.
We make a portion of our mailing list available to reputable third parties that offer products we believe may interest you. If you prefer that we not exchange your name with third parties, or if you wish to clarify or modify your communication preferences, please visit us at www.ReaderService.com/consumerchoice or write to us at Harlequin Reader Service Preference Service, P.O. Box 9062, Buffalo, NY 14269. Include your complete name and address.

LARGER-PRINT BOOKS!

**GET 2 FREE
LARGER-PRINT NOVELS
PLUS 2 FREE
MYSTERY GIFTS**

Love Inspired
SUSPENSE
RIVETING INSPIRATIONAL ROMANCE

Larger-print novels are now available...

YES! Please send me 2 FREE LARGER-PRINT Love Inspired® Suspense novels and my 2 FREE mystery gifts (gifts are worth about $10). After receiving them, if I don't wish to receive any more books, I can return the shipping statement marked "cancel." If I don't cancel, I will receive 4 brand-new novels every month and be billed just $5.24 per book in the U.S. or $5.74 per book in Canada. That's a savings of at least 23% off the cover price. It's quite a bargain! Shipping and handling is just 50¢ per book in the U.S. and 75¢ per book in Canada.* I understand that accepting the 2 free books and gifts places me under no obligation to buy anything. I can always return a shipment and cancel at any time. Even if I never buy another book, the two free books and gifts are mine to keep forever.

110/310 IDN F5CC

Name	(PLEASE PRINT)
Address	Apt. #
City	State/Prov.	Zip/Postal Code

Signature (if under 18, a parent or guardian must sign)

Mail to the **Harlequin® Reader Service:**
IN U.S.A.: P.O. Box 1867, Buffalo, NY 14240-1867
IN CANADA: P.O. Box 609, Fort Erie, Ontario L2A 5X3

**Are you a current subscriber to Love Inspired Suspense books
and want to receive the larger-print edition?
Call 1-800-873-8635 or visit www.ReaderService.com.**

* Terms and prices subject to change without notice. Prices do not include applicable taxes. Sales tax applicable in N.Y. Canadian residents will be charged applicable taxes. Offer not valid in Quebec. This offer is limited to one order per household. Not valid for current subscribers to Love Inspired Suspense larger-print books. All orders subject to credit approval. Credit or debit balances in a customer's account(s) may be offset by any other outstanding balance owed by or to the customer. Please allow 4 to 6 weeks for delivery. Offer available while quantities last.

Your Privacy—The Harlequin® Reader Service is committed to protecting your privacy. Our Privacy Policy is available online at www.ReaderService.com or upon request from the Harlequin Reader Service.

We make a portion of our mailing list available to reputable third parties that offer products we believe may interest you. If you prefer that we not exchange your name with third parties, or if you wish to clarify or modify your communication preferences, please visit us at www.ReaderService.com/consumerschoice or write to us at Harlequin Reader Service Preference Service, P.O. Box 9062, Buffalo, NY 14269. Include your complete name and address.

When helicopter pilot Creed Carter finds an abandoned baby
on a church altar, he must convince foster parent
Haley Blanchard that she'll make a good mom—and a
good match.

Baby in His Arms

by Linda Goodnight

www.LoveInspiredBooks.com

LI7824

Former gunslinger Hunter Mitchell wants to start his life over
with his newly discovered nine-year-old daughter—and his best
chance at providing his daughter a stable home is a marriage of
convenience to her beautiful and fiercely protective teacher.

Charity
HOUSE

The Outlaw's Redemption

by

RENEE RYAN

Available July 2013.

Love Inspired® SUSPENSE

RIVETING INSPIRATIONAL ROMANCE

Someone is after Tessa Camry—but only she knows why. Now she must depend on bodyguard Seth Sinclair to keep her safe from her past...and give her a reason to look forward to the future.

HEROES *for* HIRE

DEFENDER FOR HIRE

by

SHIRLEE McCoy

Available July 2013 wherever books are sold.

www.LoveInspiredBooks.com

LIS4544